unshaken

UNSHAKEN
Francine Rivers

TYNDALE HOUSE PUBLISHERS, INC.
WHEATON, ILLINOIS

Library of Congress Cataloging-in-Publication Data

Rivers, Francine, date
  Unshaken / Francine Rivers
    p. cm. — (Lineage of grace)
  ISBN 0-8423-3597-8
  1. Ruth (Biblical figure)—Fiction. 2. Bible. O.T.—History of Biblical events—Fiction.
3. Women in the Bible—Fiction.   I. Title

PS3568.I83165 U47 2001
813'.54—dc21   00-046702

Printed in United States of America

06   05   04   03   02   01
 9   8   7   6   5   4

To my mother-in-law,
Edith Rivers,
whom I admire and adore.

Thank you, Ron Beers, for sharing your vision.

Kathy Olson, thank you for fine-tuning the manuscripts

and for your acute knowledge of Scripture.

And thank you to the entire Tyndale team for your

continued support and hard work.

Special thanks to you, Scott Mendel. I appreciate the historical information,

resources, and insights you have shared with me.

Thank you, Peggy Lynch, for those brainstorming sessions

when you challenge my thinking.

Your love of the Lord and His Word is a blessing

to everyone who knows you.

And, as always, to Jane Jordan Browne. You have been

my friend and encourager from the beginning.

May the Lord bless all of you!

DEAR READER,

This is the third of five novellas on the women in the lineage of Jesus Christ. These were Eastern women who lived in ancient times, and yet their stories apply to our lives and the difficult issues we face in our world today. They were on the edge. They had courage. They took risks. They did the unexpected. They lived daring lives, and sometimes they made mistakes—big mistakes. These women were not perfect, and yet God in His infinite mercy used them in His perfect plan to bring forth the Christ, the Savior of the world.

We live in desperate, troubled times when millions seek answers. These women point the way. The lessons we can learn from them are as applicable today as when they lived thousands of years ago.

Tamar is a woman of **hope.**
Rahab is a woman of **faith.**
Ruth is a woman of **love.**
Bathsheba is a woman who received **unlimited grace.**
Mary is a woman of **obedience.**

These are historical women who actually lived. Their stories, as I have told them, are based on biblical accounts. Although some of their actions may seem disagreeable to us in our century, we need to consider these women in the context of their own times.

This is a work of historical fiction. The outline of the story is provided by the Bible, and I have started with the facts provided for us there. Building on that foundation, I have created action, dialogue, internal motivations, and in some cases, additional characters that I feel are consistent with the biblical record. I have attempted to remain true to the scriptural message in all points, adding only what is necessary to aid in our understanding of that message.

At the end of each novella, we have included a brief study section. The ultimate authority on people of the Bible is the Bible itself. I encourage you to read it for greater understanding. And I pray that as you read the Bible, you will become aware of the continuity, the consistency, and the confirmation of God's plan for the ages—a plan that includes you.

Francine Rivers

RUTH 1:1-4

In the days when the judges ruled in Israel, a man from Bethlehem in Judah left the country because of a severe famine. He took his wife and two sons and went to live in the country of Moab. The man's name was Elimelech, and his wife was Naomi. Their two sons were Mahlon and Kilion. They were Ephrathites from Bethlehem in the land of Judah. During their stay in Moab, Elimelech died and Naomi was left with her two sons. The two sons married Moabite women. One married a woman named Orpah, and the other a woman named Ruth. . . .

RUTH walked down the narrow, crowded streets of
Kir-hareseth, her mind and heart in turmoil. Her beloved
husband, Mahlon, was dying of a lingering illness that had
come upon him months earlier. She fought the sorrow and
fear stirring in her. How would she live without Mahlon?
She'd dreamed of living a long life with the man she loved,
bearing his children, growing old with him. And now, she
suffered watching him suffer. She grieved that there would
never be children to carry on his name.

But it was the new moon, and her mother was expecting
her for her monthly visit. They would drink tea, eat the
delicacies of her father's table, and talk about family matters.
Ruth dreaded this visit. She couldn't keep her mind from
her troubles. And she didn't want to hear what her mother
thought was the cause of them.

Poor Naomi! How could her mother-in-law bear another loss? Fifteen years ago she'd lost her husband, Elimelech; and her younger son, Kilion, had died last spring. Would Naomi's faith in the God of Israel continue to give her peace, or would she finally crumble beneath the crushing grief of losing her last son?

Oh, Lord God of Israel, hear our cry!

From the time Naomi had told her about the true God, she had believed because she saw such peace in her mother-in-law. It was a peace that defied circumstances. Ruth had never seen such peace, certainly not in the house of her mother and father. She and Naomi had spoken often of God, especially when questions had arisen in Ruth's heart. And the answers had always come down to trusting God, obeying Him, accepting His will, knowing there was a purpose in what was happening even if they couldn't see it. But sometimes the pain seemed unbearable.

And Ruth was afraid.

Would she be inconsolable like her sister-in-law, Orpah, had been when Kilion died last year, wailing and rocking and refusing to eat until Ruth and Naomi were afraid for her health?

Oh, Lord God, don't let me be a burden to Naomi. Give me the strength to help her.

When she reached her father's house, she took a deep breath, squared her shoulders, and knocked. A servant opened the door and smiled brightly. "Ruth! Come," she beckoned eagerly. "Come."

It was difficult to enter her father's grand house with its expensive furnishings and not make comparisons to the humble abode of her husband. Here, everywhere she looked was the conspicuous evidence of wealth—fine urns, rugs, beautifully colored linen curtains, low tables inlaid with ivory. She had grown up in this house and taken her father's wealth for granted. Then she met, fell in love with, and married a young Hebrew merchant who was having difficulty keeping the family business going and, sometimes, keeping food on the table.

Her father and mother took great pride in their possessions, but over the years of living with Naomi, Ruth had come to recognize her own parents' poverty of spirit. There was a richness in Naomi's life that had nothing to do with the house she lived in or the material possessions she had.

"Ah, my beautiful daughter." Ruth's mother entered the room and embraced her. They exchanged kisses. "Sit, my love." She clapped her hands, gave quick orders to a maiden, and sat on one of the plump scarlet-and-blue cushions. "Do you notice anything new?"

Ruth glanced around. Was there a new table or wall hanging or rug? When she looked back at her mother, she saw her fingering a gold necklace.

"What do you think? It's beautiful, isn't it? A gift from your father. It's from Egypt."

"He's always been generous," Ruth said, her mind drifting back to Mahlon. He'd insisted she come today, insisted she leave him for a while. His mother was with him. Everything was fine. *"Go. Go and enjoy yourself."* But how could she? All she could think about was Mahlon and how quickly she could leave this place and go home to him, where she belonged.

A servant entered with a tray laden with fruit, bread, two goblets, and an urn of wine. A second servant set down a platter of cooked grain with bits of roasted lamb. Ruth's stomach cramped at the tantalizing aroma of the well-seasoned food, but she didn't extend her hand, even when her mother pressed her. How could she take a bite when Mahlon was too ill to eat anything at all? How could she enjoy the delicacies her mother spread out on the table before her when her mother-in-law had nothing in the house but bread, olive oil, and sour wine?

"You must keep up your strength, Ruth," her mother said softly. "You're so thin."

"Perhaps in a while, Mother."

"Orpah's mother spoke with me in the marketplace yesterday. Has everything been done that can be done?"

Unable to speak, Ruth nodded. Naomi, insisting there was always hope, continued to pray and beseech God. She and Ruth both prayed. Prayer had become an unceasing habit.

"Oh, my darling. I'm so sorry you're going through this." Her mother reached out and placed her hand over Ruth's. For a moment, she was silent. "What will you do when he dies?"

Ruth's eyes filled with tears at the blunt question. "I will grieve. I will comfort Naomi. Beyond that, I don't know. And I can't think about it now."

"But you must."

"Mother," Ruth said softly in protest and then drew in a sobbing breath as she covered her face.

Her mother rushed on. "I didn't ask you here to cause you more pain. I know how much you love Mahlon. If your

4

father didn't love you so much, he would have insisted you marry Kasim, and you wouldn't be facing such anguish now. Your father wants you to know that you're welcome to come home. And you know how much I'd love to have you here with me again, even if only for a little while. You needn't stay with Naomi if Mahlon dies. Come back to us."

Ruth dropped her hands into her lap and stared at her mother through her tears. "After all Naomi has been through, could I leave her? My duty is to my husband's household, Mother. You know that."

"Naomi would be the first to tell you to return to us. Do you think she'll want to stay here when her last son dies? She will go home to her own people where she belongs."

The words cut into Ruth's heart. Her mother spoke as though Mahlon was already dead and Naomi best forgotten. "I must go, Mother." She started to rise.

Her mother caught her hand. "No, please, listen to me. Naomi's husband was eager to adopt our customs and become one of us, but your mother-in-law has always held herself aloof. She still dresses like a Hebrew. She's never set foot in one of our temples nor given a single offering to any one of our gods. Perhaps that's why she suffers so. Our gods are angry with her."

"She has a God of her own."

"Oh yes, and what good is he? What has he given her but poverty and grief?" She made a sweeping gesture. "Look around you, Daughter. See how the gods of Moab bless us. Look at what we have to show for *our* faith."

"But you're never satisfied, Mother."

Her eyes darkened. "I'm satisfied."

"Then why do you always want more? Possessions don't matter to Naomi."

Her mother released her hand angrily. "Of course not. Why would possessions matter to someone who will never have them?"

"You don't understand, Mother."

"I understand that you've turned away from the gods of your own people to worship hers. And what good has come from it? You're being punished for it. Turn back to the gods of our people, Ruth. Leave that house of sorrow and come home."

Home to what? Her father and mother had never been content. The more wealth her father accumulated, the more he wanted. Their appetites were ever whetted for increase. Nothing satisfied. In a few days, her mother would tire of the gold necklace she wore, and she would hunger for something new, something about which to boast.

Naomi boasted in nothing but the God of Israel. And she found peace even in the midst of chaos when she went to Him in prayer.

God, oh God, help me! There are so many things I don't understand. I have no answers for my mother. Can you hear the voice of a frightened Moabitess? I don't want my faith to die if You choose to take Mahlon from me. My mother's words are like spears in my heart. Shield me.

She wept.

"We know you must stay with Mahlon to the end, Ruth. And we understand that you'll want to stay for a few weeks after that and comfort Naomi. Fulfill your duty to her. Then come home to us, my love. Come home where you belong and where life will be so much easier for you. Everyone will understand. Naomi loves you. She'll want the best for you, just as we do. There's no need for you to live in poverty. You're young and beautiful. You have your whole life ahead of you."

But Ruth couldn't imagine her life without the man she loved or the mother-in-law who had opened her heart to her. How could staying a few weeks fulfill her obligation to Naomi? Duty was not the only bond between them. There was also love. Not just love for one another but love for the God they both believed in.

"I can't leave her, Mother."

"But what about your own family? What about your father? What about *me?* Come home, Ruth. Please come home to us. How can I bear to see you live in such poor circumstances when . . ."

Ruth felt torn between her love for her mother and father and her love for Naomi and Orpah. If Mahlon did die, could she turn her back on them and walk away? Could she go back to living the way she had before, bowing down to the statues representing the gods of her mother and father, gods she no longer believed even existed? The bond she had with Naomi was deeper than a relationship by marriage. Ruth had come to embrace her mother-in-law's beliefs in an unseen God. She had explained her new beliefs to her mother and father, and heard them laugh and shake their heads. *"How can you believe such nonsense? An unseen god?"* She loved her mother and father deeply, but she wouldn't turn her back on Naomi or the truth she had come to realize through her.

"Mahlon, Naomi, and Orpah are my family, Mother, just as Father became yours when you married him."

When her mother's face crumpled in tears, Ruth embraced her. "You know I love you, Mother. I'll always love you. But I must do what's right."

"This isn't right! You're throwing away your life!"

Ruth saw that her mother refused to understand. Things could never be the same as they had been when Ruth was a child in her father's household. She was a woman now, with a husband and a mother-in-law and responsibilities toward both. Her life didn't belong to herself anymore. And even if it did, would her decision be any different?

Oh, Lord, give me strength. I feel like a broken jar with all the oil spilling out.

She had to tell her mother the truth. It wouldn't be fair to leave her with false hopes.

"I won't leave Naomi, Mother. You have Father. You have my brothers and their wives and children, and my sisters and their families. If Mahlon does die, who will Naomi have left?"

"She will have Orpah," her mother said stubbornly. "Let Orpah stay with her."

Orpah didn't believe in the God of Israel. She still worshiped idols and burned incense to Ashtoreth. "Orpah is a kind and loving daughter-in-law, but she doesn't share Naomi's faith."

Her mother's eyes darkened in anger. "How can you persist in believing in this unseen god of hers after all that's happened? It's not fair that you give up your life for this ill-fated family! If Naomi decides to leave, *let her go!*"

Ruth refused to be drawn into another argument about whose god had grander temples or the most elaborate and pleasurable worship services. She drew back and stood. "Mahlon needs me. I must go."

Her mother rose with her, weeping again as she followed her to the door. "Please consider carefully what you're going to do, Ruth. I beg of you! Don't throw your life away!"

Ruth's emotions warred within her. Love . . . grief . . . impatience . . . confusion. She turned and embraced her mother quickly. "I love you," she said in a choked voice. "Tell Father I love him, too." She released her hold, turned away, and hurried out the door.

As she sped along the narrow city streets, she covered her face with her shawl so those passing would not see her anguish.

✦   ✦   ✦

Grief is deeper when the sun goes down and memories rise up with the moon and stars. The streets of Kir-hareseth were deserted now, everyone home and asleep, but Naomi's mind was whirring as she sat at the end of her pallet, her back against the cold stone wall of her small house. She felt alone, even though her two beloved daughters-in-law lay sleeping within a few feet of her. They were worn out with sorrow. Each had lost a husband, Orpah first and then Ruth. But they would never experience the deeper grief of losing their children, for they had none.

My sons are dead! My sons, oh, my sons . . . Naomi wanted to scream out her pain, but for the sake of the young women sleeping nearby held it in instead.

It was dark now, so dark the night closed in around

Naomi, bringing with it fear and doubt. She tried to pray, but her whispered words seemed to bounce off the ceiling and land back in her lap unheard. And she began to wonder. Had God ever heard her prayers? Had the Lord ever listened to her pleas?

Like the approach of locusts ready to feast upon her faith, the silence hummed inside her head. She pressed her hands over her ears and clenched her teeth. Why was the night like this? Sometimes the darkness was so still she could hear her own blood rushing through her veins. The sound was like a heavy rain washing open the doors of her mind, flooding her with memories she wanted to forget.

The room echoed with her dead husband's voice. "We're going to Moab whether you like it or not, Naomi! There's no famine there."

"But, Elimelech, we mustn't leave Bethlehem! It's our home."

"Our home is turning to dust!"

"If we trust and obey God, He will provide."

"Are you blind? Look around you, woman. God has abandoned us!"

"Because you and others bow down to baals!"

"I bow down to Baal because he's the lord of this land!"

"Moses told our fathers the Lord is God and there is no other!"

"And what good has God done for us lately?" Elimelech argued. "How long since rain last fell on our land? When was the last time our crops produced even a little more than what we need to fill our own stomachs?"

"But you are saying it yourself, my husband. The Lord has provided what we need to survive."

"I'm sick of hearing you say that! *I'm* the one taking care of us, Naomi. *I'm* the one working my flesh to the bones on this rocky ground and watching my crops die! Don't tell me God is taking care of us! Look at my hands! Look at the calluses and tell me it's God who takes care of you and our sons. God stands far off and watches while everything I own turns to dust. He's abandoned us! You're just a woman. What do you understand of these things? I'll do what's right in my own eyes."

That same day, Elimelech had mortgaged the land he'd inherited from his father. He'd come home, packed their possessions on two donkeys, and taken Naomi and their sons, Mahlon and Kilion, away from Bethlehem. She'd barely had time to bid good-bye to her friends and few remaining family members. Elimelech had been so certain he was making the right decision! What man wanted to hear the constant dripping of a nagging wife? So she did what she felt she could do: she kept silent with her doubts and she prayed.

She prayed in the morning when she first awakened. She prayed throughout the day as she worked. And she prayed when she lay down upon her pallet at night. She prayed and prayed and prayed—and watched her life turn to ashes.

Elimelech found work in Moab at Kir-hareseth. He cut off his locks of hair, shaved off his beard, and donned Moabite clothing to make his way easier. There were other Israelites sojourning in Moab and living in Kir-hareseth. They, too, had come to wait out the famine in the Promised Land, and they, too, quickly embraced the ways of the people around them and forgot the Law of Moses and the promises of God.

It was summer when Elimelech died.

"I just need to rest." He'd come home complaining of pain in his chest. "I'll be fine in the morning." He'd sat right where she was sitting now, rubbing his arm, up and down, up and down, grimacing. "Naomi?" The strange catch in his throat had brought her to her knees before him.

"What, my love?" She took his hand and covered it with her own, wanting to comfort him.

"Naomi," he said again, the sweat beading on his forehead. He'd looked terrified. "I only did what I thought was right." His lips were blue. She'd wanted to comfort him. She'd held him in her arms and tried to soothe him. But nothing had helped ease his torment.

Even now, after fifteen years, the grief rose up in her again, renewed by Mahlon's untimely death, just as her grief had been renewed and deepened last year when Kilion died. There was no escaping the pain, no hiding from it, no pushing it down deep inside her anymore. She remembered everything so acutely, especially her unanswered prayers. She'd prayed so hard that God wouldn't take her husband from her, prayed that God would have mercy upon him, and kept praying even as she watched the light ebb from Elimelech's eyes. Then she prayed for mercy and saw death take him.

Her sons had buried their father among Moabites. At first, she could scarcely believe Elimelech was gone. She kept thinking she would awaken from this nightmare and he would be there, complaining as always. When full realization had sunk in that she would never see him again, she had become angry with him. But that, too, passed. She had been too busy helping her sons put food on the table.

It had been fifteen years since Elimelech died, and still the grief would rise up unexpectedly. It was never as sharp as those first weeks, but it never fully dulled. She had thought the pain of losing her husband was the greatest of all, but that was before she had lost sons. Now, she was drowning in a sea of sorrow.

She couldn't even pray anymore. She had always had a glimmer of hope and a sense of God's presence. Now she felt God was beyond reach, His mercy not meant for her. All her prayers were like smoke blown away by an angry wind. Every one of them. Perhaps Elimelech had been right after all. God was standing far off, watching her suffer.

God, where are You? How do I find You?

She wanted to defend herself against His judgment. Hadn't she pleaded with her husband to stay in Bethlehem? Hadn't she begged him to trust in God? Hadn't she prayed that God would change Elimelech's mind and they would go home? Hadn't she wanted to return to Bethlehem when Elimelech died? When God had taken Elimelech, hadn't she tried desperately to convince her sons that they should go back to the land God had promised them? But Mahlon and Kilion had been old enough by then to decide for themselves.

"What is there for us, Mother? This is our home."

Their hearts had been turned away from God and the Promised Land years ago. Their home in Bethlehem was nothing more than a bad memory to them, a place of hardship and heartache. Their father had never said a good word about it. Why should her sons want to return? They knew little of Hebrew customs and laws, for Elimelech had neglected his duties. He'd never taught his sons the history of the Israelites, the Law of Moses, the way of righteousness. Her sons had watched how Elimelech lived and done as he had done. When their father died, they listened to the elders of Kir-hareseth. They listened to the priests of Chemosh. They listened to their own desires and thoughts and did as they pleased, even unto taking Moabite wives for themselves. Oh, the grief her sons had caused her!

Nothing she had said to them had mattered. They loved her, but she was just a woman. What did she know? So they said. So they'd been taught to believe by their father before them.

Naomi looked at her daughters-in-law sleeping nearby. How strange that they were her only consolation now, these young women she'd grieved over when first she heard about them. Foreign wives! The shame of Israel! Oh, how she had despaired. Yet she'd managed to put on a smiling face when Mahlon brought Ruth home, and Kilion brought Orpah. What else could she do? She could not bring herself to risk losing the love of her sons. And she'd hoped to have some small influence upon their young wives.

Now they were widows like her, and as dear to her as if they had come from her own womb. *Nothing brings people closer together than shared suffering*. She remembered in the beginning, she had accepted them and tried to build a relationship with each of them in order to keep peace in her house. And secretly, she'd prayed that Ruth's and Orpah's hearts would be softened toward the God of Israel. If she could teach them about the Lord, perhaps there would be hope for the next generation. But now her last hope for the future was lost.

A sudden fever had taken Kilion last spring. Then a lingering illness had brought Mahlon down. Kilion had died in the space of a few days, suffering little discomfort, but poor Mahlon had received no such mercy. When he fell ill, the suffering went on and on. She could do nothing but watch her eldest son, the firstfruit of Elimelech, be eaten alive by disease. She'd prayed countless times for God to ease his suffering, for God to put all the sins of her husband and sons upon her, but the days wore on and on. Poor Ruth, poor faithful, loving Ruth. How many nights had the girl sought to ease Mahlon's pain and ended up weeping over her helplessness? Sometimes Naomi wished she could escape the city and run out into the fields and scream and tear her hair and throw dust over herself. She had wept when Mahlon looked up at her with the eyes of a wounded animal in agony, hounded by terror.

Her own grief had almost consumed her during those long, terrible months, but she had spoken to Mahlon often and gently of the mercy of the Lord. *Mercy!* her heart had cried within her. *Mercy! Lord God, mercy!* While Ruth had ministered to her husband's physical needs, Naomi sat by and told him about the signs and wonders God had performed in Egypt and in the wilderness, and in the land of Canaan. He couldn't resist her now, but was he ready to repent and seek the Lord? She told Mahlon how God had delivered the Israelites from Egypt, not because they deserved it, but because He had chosen them to be His

15

people. She told him about Moses and the Law and how the people were stubborn like Elimelech and rebelled. She told him about the blessings and the cursings. And she told him about the promises. When he slept, she bowed her head and prayed. *Oh, Lord, Lord . . .* she couldn't find the words. *Oh, Lord, search my heart. . . .* She prayed and prayed and prayed.

And still Mahlon had died.

Ruth had been sitting with him and holding his hand when he died. She let out a long, anguished cry when he stopped breathing, then wailed and covered her head.

Had it been only twenty-two days ago?

Orpah had tried to comfort her and Ruth by saying Mahlon would be at peace now; his pain was over. Naomi wanted to believe these words, but they seemed hollow, without foundation. What did Orpah know of God?

Naomi's sorrow was so deep that she felt paralyzed by it. All she could do was wait for the sun to rise so she could go on sitting in this dusty, dank corner and listening to the rush of people going past her door. How dare life go on as it always had, when her sons were dead! She resented the laughter of neighbors outside her door. She was embittered by the changeless activity. Were her loved ones so unimportant they might have been mere grains of sand cast into the Dead Sea, leaving hardly a ripple? Only Orpah and Ruth shared her anguish.

Naomi hated Moab and Kir-hareseth more with each day that passed. She hated these foreign people. And she hated herself for hating them. It wasn't their fault Elimelech, Kilion, and Mahlon had taken up ways displeasing to God.

Men decide their own path, but it is God who judges, God who prevails.

The sun rose, and Naomi wished she could close her eyes and die. Instead, she found herself alive and aware of what was going on around her. She could hear Orpah and Ruth weeping together and talking in soft voices so they wouldn't disturb her. She ate when they asked her to do so and lay down when they pleaded with her to rest. But she felt lost and angry and hopeless and afraid.

She wallowed in memories, thinking back over the early years of marriage with Elimelech. Oh, how they'd laughed together and dreamed of a fine future brought by hard work and dedication to the land. Naomi, his merry one, he'd called her. She remembered the joy when she found she was with child, the anticipation, the celebration when a son was born—first one, then another. She had sustained them with her body, nursing them until they were able to walk. She had rejoiced in their childish exuberance, laughed at their antics, relished their presence. Life had been full then. She'd felt God's presence in every blessing.

What do I have now? Nothing! I will never know joy again.

Things had been bad in Bethlehem, but everything got worse when they left. She'd tried—and failed—to have influence over Elimelech. She had wanted to raise her sons in the ways of the Lord, but Elimelech felt the Laws of Moses were too rigid, too intolerant. "Our way is not the only way, Naomi. Look around you and see how the Moabites prosper. Those in Bethlehem are still reduced to scraping out a living from the earth." In her heart, she'd known Elimelech was rejecting God, but she could never find the words to convince him he must turn back.

Is that why I'm being punished? Should I have been more determined in reasoning with Elimelech? Should I have gone to the elders for help instead of being too ashamed to admit what was happening in my home? Should I have gone to his brothers? I should have found someone he respected who might have been able to dissuade him from leaving the land God gave us! Perhaps if I'd refused to leave Bethlehem, everything would have turned out differently. Perhaps if we'd stayed, my husband and sons would still be alive.

How she tormented herself wondering if she could have done things differently, worrying that she had failed those she loved so much.

Oh, why didn't I teach Kilion and Mahlon the importance of the Law? I should have been a better mother. I should have made them sit down and listen. I should have worried less about losing their love and more about losing their souls. And now I've lost them forever. I've lost my sons . . . oh, my sons, my sons . . .

She didn't speak the words aloud, but she was scourged with self-recriminations day after day and night after night.

Father, forgive me. I was weak. I was foolish. I took the easy way and followed Elimelech because I wanted peace in our family. I didn't want to be a contentious wife. I wanted to support him in his endeavors. I wanted to be his helpmate. But You warned us of the cursings to come if we were unfaithful. Oh, Father, I wanted to be faithful. I tried to be faithful. Every day, I felt torn, my husband on one side and You on the other. I didn't know what else to do but pray in silence and hope in

*secret and walk alongside Elimelech and then my sons. I hoped
and prayed every day they would come to their senses and we'd
go home to the land You gave us. Oh, God, I've prayed and
prayed all these years, and not one prayer has been answered.
My husband is dead. My sons are dead! You have stripped me
bare! You have poured me out! Who is left but You, Father?
What do I have to cling to now but You?*

She rocked back and forth, moaning.

Ruth rose and put her arms around her. "Mother, I'll take
care of you." The girl's tenderness broke Naomi's heart. She
wept in her daughter-in-law's arms, allowing herself to be
held and rocked like a baby. But it was no comfort, for other
thoughts rushed into her tortured mind and made her cry
all the harder.

There would be no children to carry on the names of her
sons. It would be as though they never lived at all. *Their
names will go down into the dust along with them. No children
. . . there will be no children. . . .*

+   +   +

Seventy days passed before Naomi went outside the door of
her small house. The sunlight hurt her eyes. She was weak
from grieving, having wept enough tears to fill a cistern,
and it was time to stop. Crying would not bring the dead
back to life. She must think of the living. Ruth and Orpah
were young women, too young to spend the rest of their
lives mourning over Mahlon and Kilion, or taking care of an
old woman whose life was over.

She sat on the stool outside her door and watched someone else's children. They raced down the street, their laughter echoing back as they rounded a corner. Children were

life, and hers were no more. But there was still a chance for her daughters-in-law, if she did what she knew she must.

If she remained in Kir-hareseth, Ruth and Orpah would continue to live with her. They would spend their youth looking after the mother of their dead husbands. How could she allow these sweet girls to waste their lives on her? She loved them too much to continue to see them begging for a handful of grain from strangers or living off charity from friends and relatives. But if she left Kir-hareseth and Moab, her daughters-in-law could return to their families, who would welcome them. Naomi had no doubt their fathers would find husbands for them quickly, for they were young and beautiful. Then Ruth and Orpah would have the joy of children. Naomi wanted that for them more than anything.

As for her, she wanted to go home to Bethlehem. She didn't know if any of her relatives or friends remained there or had survived the famine, but she had heard that the famine had finally ended. Perhaps the Midianite raids had also come to an end. Even so, what did it matter? She longed to go home, and she was willing to accept whatever she found when she reached Bethlehem. If she must be reduced to spending her last years as a beggar, so be it. At least she would feel the Promised Land beneath her feet again. At least she would be where others worshiped God as she did.

Oh, Lord, make it be so. Bring me safely home before I die. Oh, Father, have mercy on me, for I'm alone and in deep distress. My problems go from bad to worse. And I want to do what's right in Your eyes. Help me!

Neighbors greeted her as they passed by. She smiled and nodded her head while her mind raced on. *Why am I sitting here? Am I waiting for God to speak to me audibly as He did to Moses? Who am I that God would speak in such a manner? Do I expect Him to write a letter to me on that wall over there telling me what to do? I know what I must do! I will repent and return to my homeland.*

Naomi put her hands on her knees and pushed herself up. Lowering her shawl to her shoulders, she went back into her house. Ruth was kneeling, flattening bread dough and laying it over the metal stove, while Orpah was mending a garment. Both young women glanced up and smiled at her. She paused, gazing between them, trying to find words to explain, and failing. She turned away and began gathering her few things.

Ruth rose. "What are you doing, Mother?"

"I'm packing."

"Packing?" Orpah said. "But where are you going?"

"I'm going home."

✦   ✦   ✦

Naomi had known that Ruth and Orpah would insist on accompanying her to Bethlehem. Impetuous youth. She didn't argue with them; she knew they would soon understand the immensity of leaving Moab and their families behind. She was sure they would be ready to go home again by the time they reached the Arnon River. It would be far easier to dissuade them at the boundary of their country than to waste her breath arguing with them now. She would enjoy their company awhile longer and then send them home. She didn't want to ponder the fact that she would never see them again after they left her. She would never forget them, and she would pray for them every day for as long as she lived.

As they prepared to leave the house, Naomi wondered if they would even make it down the hill with all the things Orpah had decided to bring. The poor girl. She couldn't bear to leave anything behind. She was loaded down with everything she had accumulated during her marriage to Kilion, including a small stool. Orpah moaned in distress. "Oh, I wish we could bring the table and rug . . ."

Ruth, on the other hand, had only a pack full of colorful sashes she'd made, a skin of water, and enough grain and raisin cakes to last for several days. "Where are the rest of your things, Ruth?" Naomi asked her.

"I have all I need. Let me carry the cooking pan, Mother. It's too heavy for you. We'll travel farther today if I carry it."

Naomi had spoken to the family next door, telling them Orpah and Ruth would be returning in a day or two. She wanted to be sure no one bothered what was left in the house. When the young women returned to Kir-hareseth, they could sell everything, including the house, and split whatever came of it. Naomi didn't care about any of the belongings she was leaving behind. She preferred the plain things of her people to the finery of the Moabites, Philistines, and Egyptians. It was Elimelech who had placed such importance on the gifts he gave her, and they would be out of place in Bethlehem.

She suspected that Ruth would give everything to Orpah. Dear Ruth—she had such a generous heart, not to mention a wealthy father who would want her to return to his house. Naomi knew him well enough to suspect that he already had another husband in mind for Ruth, a rich merchant's son or an official in the king's court. Her heart sank at the thought of Ruth married to someone other than her son. Curious . . . the same wasn't true of Orpah.

Perhaps it was because Ruth had responded to her teachings about the true God. How Naomi had rejoiced as she watched the slow budding of the girl's faith.

"Did you see your father and mother yesterday, Ruth?"

Ruth shook her head.

"Why not? They should know you're leaving the city."

"They will know that I'm with you."

"Do they know I'm going back to Bethlehem?"

"My mother said you would, and I told her that even if you did, I belong with my husband's family."

Naomi said no more about it. She started off, carrying only a small sack of parched grain, a skin of water, and a leather bag in which was a sandalwood box containing crystals of frankincense. She would give it to the priest when she reached Bethlehem, an offering for the Lord.

She felt a sense of relief as she walked through the gates of Kir-hareseth and saw the road before her. Whatever hardships came, at least she was on her way back to Canaan. She didn't look back. Orpah did look back, weeping softly, but Ruth merely smiled and gazed off toward the King's Highway to the Dead Sea. "It's a good day to begin our journey, Mother."

The day wore on and the sun rose, hot and oppressive. Naomi felt despair creeping into her heart. Soon she would say good-bye to these daughters. *Lord, give me the strength to place their needs ahead of my fear of being alone. Father,*

*bless them for their kindness to me. Take them safely home,
and give me the courage to go on alone.*

At midday they stopped to rest beneath a terebinth tree.
Naomi accepted the raisin cake and cup of water Ruth
offered, but Orpah declined food. She was quiet, her eyes
downcast. Ruth sat down and wiped the perspiration from
her face. She looked weary but was more concerned about
her sister-in-law than herself. "Are you not feeling well,
Orpah?"

"I'll be all right after a rest."

Naomi knew what was wrong, but the knowledge gave
her no satisfaction. She must send them back now. There
was still time enough for them to be safely back inside the
city walls before nightfall. She finished eating quickly and
rose, lifting to her own back the bundle Ruth had insisted
upon carrying to this point.

"What are you doing?" Ruth said, rising as well.

"I'm going on alone."

"No, Mother!"

Orpah came to her feet and joined Ruth in protest, weeping profusely. "Don't go! Please don't go."

Naomi's heart broke, but she knew she must remain firm.
"Go back to your mothers' homes instead of coming with
me. And may the Lord reward you for your kindness to
your husbands and to me. May the Lord bless you with the
security of another marriage."

Ruth wept. "No." She shook her head. "No, *no* . . ." She
stepped forward. "We want to go with you to your people."

"Why should you go on with me?" Naomi said, striving
and failing to keep her voice from becoming strident with

restrained emotion. "Can I still give birth to other sons who could grow up to be your husbands? No, my daughters, return to your parents' homes, for I am too old to marry again. And even if it were possible, and I were to get married tonight and bear sons, then what? Would you wait for them to grow up and refuse to marry someone else? No, of course not, my daughters! Things are far more bitter for me than for you, because the Lord Himself has caused me to suffer."

Ruth and Orpah wept harder. Orpah embraced her. "I shall never forget you, Naomi. May you have a safe journey home."

"Nor I you," Naomi said and kissed her. "And a safe journey to you as well!"

Orpah took up her bundles and started back toward Kir-hareseth. She paused after a little way and looked back, perplexed. "Aren't you coming, Ruth?"

"No." Ruth shook her head, her eyes awash with tears. "I'm going with Mother."

Orpah dropped her things and ran back to embrace her. "Are you certain, my sister?"

"Never more certain."

"Please . . ."

"No. Go back without me. I will go on with Naomi."

With one last look back, Orpah started off again. Naomi watched Orpah walk quickly away and then looked at Ruth. She stretched out her hand and pointed toward Kir-hareseth. "See. Your sister-in-law has gone back to her people and to her gods. You should do the same."

Tears slipped down Ruth's face, but she didn't move. "Don't ask me to leave you and turn back, for I won't."

"But how can I not tell you to go?" Naomi came closer. "You heard what I said, Ruth. Should I take you back to Bethlehem with me so you can have the same bitter existence I'll have? Should you grow old without a husband and children? Go after Orpah! Return to your mother and father!"

"No," Ruth said, weeping. "I *won't* leave you. Make me your proselyte."

Naomi's heart squeezed tight. "Oh, my sweet one, think of what you're saying. The lives of my people are not as easy as what you've known. We're commanded to keep Sabbaths and holy days, on which we may not travel more than two thousand cubits."

"I will go wherever you go."

Naomi knew she must speak the truth, even if it hurt Ruth's feelings. "We're commanded not to spend the night with Gentiles."

"I will live wherever you live."

"We're commanded to keep over six hundred precepts!"

"Whatever your people keep I will keep, Mother, for your people will be my people."

Naomi kept on. "We are forbidden to worship any strange god. Chemosh is an abomination!"

"Your God will be my God."

Naomi spread her hands. "We have four sorts of deaths for malefactors, Ruth: stoning, burning, strangling, and slaying with the sword. Reconsider your words!" When Ruth said nothing, she went on, beseeching Ruth to see the many ways their people were different. "Our people are buried in houses of sepulchre."

"Then let it be so for me as well, Mother." Falling to her knees, Ruth wrapped her arms around Naomi's waist. "I will die where you die and will be buried there." When Naomi tried to press her back, Ruth clung more tightly. "And may the Lord punish me severely if I allow anything but death to separate us!"

Weeping now, Naomi placed her hands on Ruth's head and stroked her hair. Naomi looked up at the heavens. She had never hoped for this, never expected that this young Moabitess would be willing to give up everything in order to go with her. She looked down again, stroking Ruth's head absently. "You will never see your mother and father and brothers and sisters again, Ruth. Do you realize that?"

"Yes." Ruth raised her head. Her face was streaked with tears.

"Your life will be easier if you return."

"Oh, Naomi, how can I go back to my old life when you hold the words of truth?" Her arms tightened again as she began to sob. "Please don't plead with me to leave you. Don't lead me into temptation. I'm going with you!"

"Your God will be my God."

How could Naomi say no to such words? Hadn't she prayed that Ruth's heart would be softened toward the God of Israel? One prayer had been answered, one prayer among thousands. "Be at ease," she said gently and loosened Ruth's arms from around her waist. Cupping Ruth's face, she smiled down at her. She smoothed away Ruth's tears. "As God wills. Whatever comes, we'll face together."

Ruth's eyes shone as she smiled in relief. "I will heed your every word, for I know you'll teach me what I need to know."

"Everything I learned at my mother's knee I will make known to you. All I have is yours. I give it to you with pleasure." For Naomi knew now there was more than marriage to her son that had grafted this girl into her life and heart. And now she would pray that Ruth would be grafted in among her people as well.

You have not forgotten me, Lord. You knew I couldn't make it home alone. You have not abandoned me.

"Come," Naomi said, taking Ruth's hand and helping her up. "We must make a long journey before we reach home."

+   +   +

Ruth didn't dwell on what hardships she and Naomi might encounter when they reached Bethlehem. Each day of travel was enough trouble to bear without fearing what might come when they reached their destination. Ruth had lived in fear all during the months of Mahlon's illness, and it had accomplished nothing. She'd loved her husband, but she couldn't save him. All her efforts to make him better had failed, and the fear of losing him hadn't prevented death from coming anyway. Nor had fear helped her face the difficulties of surviving without a man to provide for the household. After Mahlon's death, she decided she would never again allow her mind to dwell on things beyond her control. The future was one of these things. She would face whatever came and do the best with whatever life God gave her.

Naomi often comforted her without even realizing it. "The Lord will take care of us," she'd said last night, and Ruth had lain awake on the hard earth, staring up at the stars and thinking about those words. *The Lord will take care of us.* After all Naomi had suffered, she still clung to her faith. Ruth was comforted by Naomi's strength. *The Lord will take care of us.* She chose to believe it because her mother-in-law said it was true.

From the time she had entered Mahlon's home, Ruth had known there was something different about Naomi. First there was the outward sign: her clothing. Even after years of living among the Moabites, her mother-in-law continued to dress as a Hebrew. She didn't do so with an air of pride, as though she was better than those living around her. It was simply who she was. Ruth had also seen her deep faith in God. At first, she'd worried that Naomi's long silences meant she didn't like Mahlon's choice of a wife. But Mahlon had said that wasn't so.

"She's just praying," Mahlon had told her with a shrug. "She's done it for as long as I can remember. Don't let it upset you. It doesn't do any harm. Just ignore her."

But Ruth hadn't ignored her mother-in-law. She could see that prayer meant a great deal to Naomi, and Ruth wanted to understand more about it. So she had surreptitiously watched Naomi. Sometimes her mother-in-law would look so peaceful when she talked to her god, and at other times, anguished. Every morning, often at midday, and always during the evening hours, Naomi would draw her shawl over her head, sit in the corner of the house, and become still and quiet. Ruth asked her once what she prayed about, and Naomi had smiled and said, "Everything." Her eyes had grown sad. "Mostly about my sons." She'd reached out and put her hand over Ruth's, her eyes softening. "And my daughters."

The kind words had brought tears to Ruth's eyes. Naomi's good opinion had mattered very much, for Ruth admired her greatly. Naomi was kind and pleasant, fair in her division of chores, and she always worked as hard as everyone else. She loved both of her sons deeply and equally, and despite their cultural differences, she embraced Ruth and Orpah as daughters. Love was a gift Naomi had in abundance. And though Mahlon seemed unimpressed, Ruth sensed a deep, abiding knowledge and wisdom in her mother-in-law, knowledge and wisdom she longed to share.

Yet Ruth sensed her sorrow as well. Naomi was never quite settled in Kir-hareseth, never quite at ease with the world around her. It had to do with her God. Ruth had been afraid to approach Naomi and talk with her about it. So she approached her husband instead.

Mahlon had never had much to say about the God of his people. In fact, he seemed to know very little about Him. "Why are you so interested in God?"

"Shouldn't I be able to teach your sons about Him?"

"Teach them about Chemosh if it pleases you. It doesn't matter to me. I'm sure my mother will teach them about Yahweh. The important thing is for them to be tolerant of all religions. That's the only way they're going to succeed in Kir-hareseth."

In Mahlon's eyes, one god was no better than any other, but Naomi could not compromise. She was respectful, never disdaining others' beliefs, but she held to her faith in Yahweh with quiet tenacity.

Ruth looked at her mother-in-law now, curled on her side, her head resting on a stone for a pillow. She'd fallen asleep within minutes after eating the bread Ruth prepared for her. The sun was down and the air was cooling quickly. Ruth rose and carefully draped her shawl over Naomi. The journey was already very difficult for her mother-in-law. She had eaten very little during the weeks following Mahlon's death. Ruth had feared that Naomi would waste away in grief. So she had prepared savory stews in an effort to entice her mother-in-law's appetite. Now it was the physical exhaustion that dampened Naomi's appetite. She was so tired after walking all day, she could barely keep her eyes open long enough to eat anything. It was strange, but Ruth felt as though they had traded positions. Naomi had become the child, and she the caring mother. "But I don't mind," she whispered, leaning down to kiss Naomi's cheek. She smoothed the tendrils of black hair back from her mother-in-law's sunburned brow.

Ruth rose and hugged her arms close to her body, shivering slightly. Mount Nebo stood in the distance. Naomi had told her this morning that Moses had gone up onto that mountain and died there after putting Joshua in charge of God's people. They had crossed the Jordan River soon afterward and claimed Canaan. She loved it when Naomi talked about what God had done for the Hebrews. She felt a strange stirring within her as she learned of His mighty feats and His unfailing love.

She closed her eyes and lifted her face to the heavens. "Lord, help me to take care of Your servant Naomi," she whispered. "It's because of her that I've come to believe in

You. Please guide our steps and bring us safely home to Bethlehem. And, Lord, if it isn't too much to ask, let there be old friends to greet Naomi upon her return, people who loved her in days gone by and who will continue to love her in the difficult days ahead."

THE days were long and hot and dry. Ruth rose early and awakened Naomi. "The sun's coming up, Mother," she would say. "We should travel now in the cool of the day." Silently, they would walk until the sun reached its zenith and then find shade where they could rest. Weary, Naomi usually dozed. Ruth more often looked off down the road, wondering what the future held for both of them.

They reached the Wadi Arnon, which marked the southern boundary of the Reubenite territory, and followed the King's Highway to Dibon, Heshbon, and Abel Shittim. In each city they passed through, Ruth bartered her woven sashes in the marketplace to buy food, while inquiring about the road ahead.

"Oh, you're not going over the Jericho road," said a woman selling onions and garlic. "Robbers hide out up there in the mountains and attack the caravans. You won't be safe alone."

"I'm not alone. I'm traveling with my mother-in-law."

"Two women? Well, you'd better go down to the camel market and see if you can find a traveling merchant who will allow you to travel with his caravan. No one travels the Jericho road without protection. You'd find yourself snatched up and sold into slavery."

When Ruth returned to their little camp near the city wall, she found Naomi cooking unleavened bread on the metal bowl placed over the fire. She turned the bread skillfully with a two-pronged stick. "I've been worried," Naomi said without looking up.

"I'm sorry, Mother," Ruth said, hunkering down. "I should have come back and told you what I was doing. A woman in the marketplace told me robbers attack people going over the mountains, so I thought it wise to seek assistance. We're going to join a caravan tomorrow morning and travel with it over the Jericho road. The man is a Benjaminite, and he has armed guards. We'll be safe with him."

Naomi's body relaxed. She hooked the edge of the bread and lifted it from the bowl, laying it aside to cool. "I should have thought of that myself." She sat back on her heels and covered her face.

Ruth took the bread and broke it. She handed Naomi half. Naomi shook her head. "You must eat, Mother. You need your strength."

Hands still covering her face, Naomi wept. "Why didn't I think of the dangers? I never even considered what could happen to you. What was I thinking to let you come on this journey? I'm a selfish old woman!"

"You tried to turn me back," Ruth said with a smile. "It did you no good. Try not to worry. We're going to be safe."

Naomi raised her head. "There's more danger for a young woman like you than an old widow like me."

"There's danger for both of us, and we're taking every precaution. The man seems trustworthy."

"No one can be trusted these days."

Ruth picked up the bread and held it out to her again. Naomi took it and broke off a little piece, eating slowly, still frowning.

Ruth smiled at her. "How often have I heard you say 'the Lord watches over those who love Him'?"

"And punishes those who reject Him." Naomi's eyes welled with tears, and Ruth knew she was thinking of Elimelech, Kilion, and Mahlon. Her own grief rose sharply as she thought of her husband. He'd been so young, with years ahead of him. How she wished she'd given him a child! A son to carry on his name.

"I'm so tired," Naomi said, her voice tear-choked. "I don't know if I can even make it home. Those mountains, I remember them so well now. How could I have forgotten how hard the journey was?"

"We will rest when we need to."

"And the caravan will go on without us," Naomi said dismally.

"Then we'll join another."

"If we aren't robbed and—"

"Don't!" Ruth said with a sob. She rose and went to

Naomi, kneeling down and taking her mother-in-law's hand. "Don't even think of such things, Mother. If you do, we're defeated. Think about what's on the other side of the mountains: *Bethlehem*. Our home. If we dwell on all the things that could go wrong, we'll be too afraid to take another step. *Please*. Tell me about the Lord again, Mother. Tell me how He fed thousands of people in the desert. Tell me how He brought water from a rock. And pray." She wept softly. "Pray He has mercy upon us."

Naomi winced, her expression filled with regret. She touched Ruth's face. "Sometimes I forget." Her eyes were still awash with tears. "I think about what I've lost instead of thinking about what I have."

"We have each other," Ruth said. "And we have God. That's more than enough to face whatever comes. You taught me that."

"Keep reminding me."

✦ ✦ ✦

They crossed the Jordan River with the caravan late the next afternoon. Naomi wilted beneath the trees on the other side. "I can't go any farther."

Ruth settled her comfortably and brought some water. "Rest here while I thank Ashir Ben Hadar." The last of the camels were crossing the river when Ruth approached the caravan owner and bowed her face to the ground. "Thank you for allowing us to travel in your company."

"You're leaving the caravan so soon?"

"My mother-in-law has gone as far as her strength can carry her. We'll camp here by the river and continue on in the morning."

"A pity. We'll be camping for the night at the oasis. You'd be safer with us."

"May the Lord bring you safely to your destination and bless you for your kindness toward two widows."

He frowned heavily. "May the Lord protect you." Turning away, he mounted his camel, whacked the animal's neck with a stick, and shouted orders in Egyptian to one of his servants. The camel rocked forward and then back as it came to its feet. Ruth bowed again as the man rode toward the front of his caravan. She'd almost reached the trees by the river when one of Ashir Ben Hadar's servants ran up to her and thrust a sack and a bulging skin into her hands. "Gifts from the master," he rasped and raced off again.

Smiling, Ruth knelt down by Naomi. "Taste and see how the Lord provides for those who love Him."

Tipping the skin cautiously, Naomi took a small sip. Her eyes grew wide. "Fresh goat's milk!"

Ruth laughed and opened the leather, displaying the fullness of their bounty. "And raisin cakes, Mother. Enough for several days. With the grain we have left, we have enough to sustain us until we reach Bethlehem."

They ate and then rested as the sun slipped over the mountains behind Jericho. "It wasn't far from here that the Lord rolled back the water of the Jordan so that Joshua could bring our people across," Naomi said, replete and relaxed. "My mother told me when Moses went up Mount Nebo to Pisgah Peak and died, the people mourned for thirty days. Joshua was filled with the Spirit of God and led the people over there," she said and pointed from Nebo along the way they had come, "to Acacia. He waited there until the Lord told him what to do. Joshua brought the people to the banks of the Jordan. The Lord rolled back the water, and the people crossed on dry land. My mother and father were among the people who came into Canaan that day. They camped at Gilgal and celebrated the Passover."

Ruth was standing beneath the shade following with her eyes the course Naomi said her people had taken. "What are the stones over there?"

"The standing stones?" Naomi rose. "Everyone who passes by them will remember what the Lord did for His people. There are twelve, each stone carried by a member of one of the tribes who descended from our father, Jacob. Do you see where the water ripples over there? There are twelve more stones on the spot where the priests stood with the Ark of the Covenant while our people crossed over." She stood beside Ruth, pointing back the way they had come. "Over there is the altar the sons of Reuben, Gad, and Manasseh built. The tribes on this side almost went to war over it."

"Why?"

"Because the tribes on the west bank thought it to be an altar for burnt offerings and sacrifices to other gods. But it stands as witness that the tribes of Reuben, Gad, and Manasseh have an inheritance in the Lord; it is a monument to remind us that we are brothers."

Naomi repeated the stories her father and mother had told her, until the sun went down and the stars shone. Ruth listened hungrily to everything Naomi said about the years in the desert and the mighty deeds the Lord had done to save and discipline His people. When Naomi fell asleep, Ruth looked up into the heavens and felt reassured. Surely if the Lord had watched over His rebellious people in the wilderness, He would watch over Naomi now. Ruth believed that the Lord would bring them both safely home to Bethlehem.

The next day they walked as far as the oasis and spent the night beneath the palms. The jagged silhouette of Jericho stood out against the base of the mountains, the once-great city now blackened rubble inhabited only by lizards and snakes. However, there was a small but thriving community not far away, encamped around the spring. They earned a prosperous living from travelers using the Jericho road across the mountains to Jerusalem.

As they began the arduous journey up the Jericho road, Ruth prayed continuously, while keeping watch for dangers along the way. *God, protect us. Watch over us and guide our steps.*

A caravan came up behind them. Ruth spoke with the overseer and was given permission to camp near them the first night. She made no effort to hurry Naomi the next morning, but set her pace by her mother-in-law, even though the caravan went ahead and disappeared from sight.

"Lord, please help us get over these mountains," she whispered each night before she closed her eyes.

And each day the road was steeper and more difficult, the days hotter and their supplies shorter. Naomi weakened, so Ruth took her load. When her mother-in-law became despondent, Ruth asked her questions about Bethlehem and her childhood, hoping to revive her determination to reach their destination. "Each day we're closer, Mother."

"And what awaits us? Everyone I knew may be gone by now."

"Perhaps there will be friends you've forgotten."

"And who have forgotten me." She wept as she often did when she was close to complete exhaustion. "I'm bringing you home to poverty. There will be no one to welcome us." She covered her face and sobbed.

"Look back and see how far we've come," Ruth said, breathing hard beneath her burdens.

"Look how far we've yet to go. Up, up, forever up."

Ruth looked around. There was no place to camp where they were. They had no choice but to go on. She was close to crying along with Naomi. Her back ached from carrying the full load all day, her eyes were gritty and her throat parched. She clasped the small bottle she wore on a cord around her neck. It was filled with tears she had shed for Mahlon, a sign of her respect and love. Letting go of it, she shut her eyes tightly. "The Lord sees our sorrow, Mother. He knows our needs."

"Then where is He?"

Ruth pressed her lips together to keep from crying out in frustration and despair. She couldn't allow herself to give in to it. If she did, where would they be?

"I can't go on, Ruth. It's too hard. I can't. Just leave me here to die. I don't care anymore. I'm too tired to care!"

Ruth shifted the packs and looped her arm around Naomi, giving her support. "You have to go on. Just a little way. We'll find a place and rest for the night."

"I'll be just as tired in the morning. I'm sick and tired."

"We'll make it, Mother."

"And what will be there if we do?" Naomi said bitterly, feet dragging as she leaned heavily upon Ruth. "I have no land. I have no house. I have no husband, no sons. What will be there for us?"

Fighting tears, Ruth said, "I don't know, but whatever it is, God will help us."

After that, she could speak no more. She had only strength enough to keep them moving until they found a place of rest. *Oh, please, God, please help us!*

As they came around a bend in the road, Ruth noticed a large crack in the stone mountainside. "Just a few more feet," she said, urging Naomi on. The crevice was large enough to shelter both women for the night.

Naomi sank down with a groan and leaned back against a boulder. Ruth winced as she shrugged off her bundles and sat beside her. She rolled her shoulders to ease her aching muscles. "We're almost to the summit," she said, leaning her head back against the cold stone. "We will reach Jerusalem tomorrow."

Naomi said nothing. She was breathing heavily, her eyes closed, her face pale with exhaustion.

Ruth rose again and unrolled the bedding. She broke the last raisin cake in half. "You'll feel better after you've had something to eat." Naomi took the food and ate slowly. Ruth saw the sheen of tears in Naomi's eyes.

"God willing, we will be in Bethlehem early tomorrow," Naomi said, folding her hands in her lap. "It is only a short distance beyond Jerusalem."

Ruth smiled and put her hand over Naomi's. "You're almost home, Mother."

Naomi closed her eyes, but not before tears slipped down her dusty cheeks. Ruth sat closer and put her arm around her mother-in-law. Naomi leaned her head against Ruth's shoulder, and within moments was asleep.

Lord, Lord . . . Ruth didn't know what to pray anymore. She was too weary to think but not to fear. *Thank You for bringing us this far. Please do not leave us now.*

Ruth knew the real trial of her strength was only just beginning. With each day of travel, Naomi had become increasingly dependent upon her. Ruth did not mind, but she was plagued by worries.

What would become of them when they reached Bethlehem?

WITH Bethlehem so close, Naomi became eager to reach home. Rising before the sun, the two women set out on the final leg of their journey. Naomi's strength was renewed. Ruth didn't have to urge her on as before. "It's not far now. Not far at all," Naomi said. With the rising sun, they followed the road past Jerusalem. It was still morning when they entered the town of Bethlehem. Women were gathered at the well in the center of town, talking and laughing as they drew up water for the day's household needs. They noticed Naomi and Ruth, and drew in closer together, lowering their voices. Ruth could feel Naomi's tension. "Come, Mother. Perhaps there will be someone you know, and I need to fill the skins."

One woman, older than the rest, separated herself from

the others. "Is it really Naomi?" She frowned heavily, tilting her head as though she couldn't see clearly.

Ruth touched her mother-in-law's arm gently. "You aren't forgotten. You still have friends in Bethlehem."

"It is Naomi!" She came toward her, arms outstretched. "Naomi, you have returned!"

The women cried out in excitement, hastening toward her mother-in-law. Ruth stepped back to allow them room, giving silent thanks to God that Naomi was remembered and welcomed so warmly. Perhaps the enthusiastic greeting of these women would raise her mother-in-law's spirits.

"Naomi, you look as though you've traveled hundreds of miles!"

"Where have you been all these years?"

"We heard you went to Moab."

"What's happened to you?"

Ruth saw Naomi's distress growing. Her mother-in-law looked this way and that as though seeking an escape from this throng of interrogators.

"I remember the day you left with mules loaded down with your possessions."

"What's happened to you?"

Ruth could only imagine what her mother-in-law was thinking. Naomi was home in Bethlehem, but she was destitute. She was among friends but was clearly the object of their pity and curiosity. Aching for her, Ruth was uncertain what to do. Should she press her way into the center of the circle and try to rescue her? Or would that only make matters worse? The women had made a tight circle around Naomi, while presenting Ruth their backs. In fact, no one had given her more than a hostile glance. The women made no effort to hide their shock at Naomi's appearance.

"Where is your husband, Elimelech?"

"Such a tall, handsome man."

The women pressed in upon Naomi from all sides, asking questions that would only stir up the grief of recent tragedies.

"You had sons. Where are they?"

"Surely they haven't remained in Moab!"

"Where are Mahlon and Kilion?"

They were all speaking at once, their piqued interest focused on Naomi's misery. Ruth was not surprised or hurt because the women chose to ignore her. Naomi had warned her she would not be welcome. "My people will see you as a foreigner. And worse, they'll know you're a Moabitess." Everything about Ruth's appearance declared her nationality. Her clothing was distinctive, and her skin was darker. She had no money to change the one, and no ability to change the other. It would take time for these people to accept her.

"Don't expect to be invited into anyone's house," Naomi had said. A Hebrew could not invite a foreigner inside his home without defiling it.

"Oh, Naomi," the women said, hearing about the death of Elimelech, Kilion, and Mahlon. "Oy, your sorrow is too much to bear!" They seemed to withdraw slightly, embarrassed, uncertain. Were they afraid Naomi's misfortune might somehow be transferred to them if they offered her assistance? Ruth moved forward, edging her way through the women until she was close enough to Naomi to be seen.

"Don't call me Naomi." Naomi cried out. "Instead, call me Mara, for the Almighty has made life very bitter for me." She began to weep and wail. "I went away full, but the Lord has brought me home empty. Why should you call me Naomi when the Lord has caused me to suffer and the Almighty has sent such tragedy?"

Perhaps the women had been too long separated from Naomi to share her grief. Though offering words of sympathy, they seemed ill equipped to comfort her. They stood uneasy, looking at one another, distressed and silent. Ruth moved forward again, and when Naomi's gaze fell upon her, relief flooded her mother-in-law's face. "Ruth, oh, my Ruth, come here to me."

As Ruth pressed her way forward, the women moved back from her, drawing away so she wouldn't brush against them. They no longer ignored her, but stared openly, contemptuously. Heat poured into Ruth's cheeks. Had the Moabites stared at Naomi the same way when she first came to Kir-hareseth?

"This is my daughter-in-law. This is Mahlon's widow, Ruth," Naomi said, taking her hand. Ruth could feel how Naomi was shaking. Was this the moment her mother-in-law had most dreaded? Introducing her Moabitess daughter-in-law to her friends? Was Naomi ashamed of her? She was all the proof these people needed that at least one of Naomi's sons had turned away from God and taken a foreign wife. Ruth was filled with sorrow at the thought of causing her mother-in-law more grief.

"She's a Moabite." The words came out like a curse.

"By birth," Naomi said.

"Does she expect to stay here?" Never had Ruth felt so unwelcome.

Naomi lifted her chin, her hand tightening around Ruth's. "Yes, she will stay. She and I will live together."

"But Naomi, think of what you're doing!"

"I would not have survived without Ruth."

"You're among your own people now, Naomi. Send the foreigner back where she belongs. You know what the Law says."

Naomi turned slightly, her body rigid. "There were Egyptians who came with us out of Egypt."

"And look at the trouble they caused!"

"Foreign women are cursed of God!"

"They turn our men's hearts away from the Lord!"

"Enough!" Naomi cried out. "Should I cut off what God has grafted in? Ruth chose to come with me. She turned her back on her mother and father and her brothers and sisters, all she has ever known, to come to Bethlehem and worship God with me."

Everyone fell silent for a moment, but Ruth knew words could not convince these women that she was worthy of acceptance. She would have to live an exemplary life before them in order for them to believe she had chosen Naomi over her father and mother, and God over the idols of her people. Time. It would take time.

"You have returned in time for Passover, Naomi. It is good to have you back among us."

And with that said, the women began to disperse, leaving Ruth and Naomi alone at the well.

Ruth wept softly. "I have brought shame upon you. I have

made your homecoming even more difficult than it might have been otherwise."

"No," Naomi said wearily. "They remember the way I was before I left. My husband prospered and I had cause to rejoice. I could laugh and sing with them. Now my wretchedness makes them uncomfortable. If it could happen to me, they think, it could happen to them. It's not a comforting thought."

"You will laugh and sing with them again, Mother."

Naomi shook her head. "I didn't expect to find anyone," she said softly. "But this . . ." She bent her neck, staring down at the ground. "Not one offered us so much as a loaf of bread or a sip of watered wine."

"Because of me."

"Should you take all the blame? I lived in Moab for twenty years. I dwelt among idol worshipers and opened my home to the foreign women my sons took for wives. In Hebrew eyes, I am as defiled as you. Perhaps more so because I *knew better*." Naomi's eyes welled with tears. "Oh, my dear. You're all I have. You're God's blessing to me. We are not going to be welcome in their homes, Ruth. It is the way things are. We will have to make our own way." Tears spilled down her cheeks. "And tomorrow is Passover. I'd forgotten. How could I forget a day so important? The most important celebration of my people and I . . ."

Ruth embraced her. She held Naomi close, stroking her as she would a hurt child, all the while aware of several women watching them from their doorways. When Naomi regained control over her emotions, Ruth kept a protective arm around her. "We will find someplace to stay, Mother. Everything will look better after a good night's sleep."

Ruth took a coin from the small cache she kept deep in her pack, but when she offered it to an innkeeper on the edge of town, he shook his head. "There's no room in the inn for you."

As Ruth turned away, she saw how haggard and dejected Naomi looked. Truly, Naomi was "Mara," for Ruth had never seen her look so bitter. "We will go on," Ruth said. There will be another place farther down the road."

But there wasn't. As the morning wore on, Ruth realized there would be no room for them anywhere in Bethlehem. "We have slept under the stars before," she said, trying to remain hopeful for her mother-in-law's sake.

"The land that belonged to my husband is not far from here," Naomi said as they walked beyond the borders of the town. "There are caves near it. The shepherds use them as folds for their sheep during the winter months, but the flocks will be gone by now. They will have contracts with the landowners to graze in the fields after harvest."

The larger caves were still occupied by members of the shepherds' families. Leaving a cave unattended was an open invitation for the destitute to take residence. But not far away was another cave that was empty, one not large enough to be of use as a sheepfold, but more than big enough to shelter two tired, lonely women from the elements. Naomi entered and looked around as Ruth unpacked their bedding and few possessions.

The difficult days of travel were over, but Ruth could see her mother-in-law's grief was deeper and more acute now than it had been during the grueling days of their journey. All the years her mother-in-law had dreamed of coming home, only to find herself here in such mean surroundings with nothing but the clothes on her back and a few necessities for survival—cookstove, blanket, water. Night was falling. It was going to be cold. They had little food left and no relative to show pity on them.

Naomi moved farther into the cave and sat with her back against the stone, staring into the shadows. Her face was filled with despair. Ruth wondered if she was thinking back to the way things had been before she and her husband and sons left this city. Were regret and guilt being added to grief over her losses?

"I went away full, but the Lord has brought me home empty . . ." she'd said at the well.

Ruth looked out and wondered what it had been like when Mahlon was a little boy. Memories of her husband flooded her. Poor Mahlon. He'd been so young when he died, all his hopes and dreams dying with him. And there would be no son to carry on his name. But she could not allow herself to dwell upon these thoughts. It would only weaken her and make her of no use to Naomi, who needed her desperately. Being needed and of use was a good thing.

She drew in her breath. "It's spring, Mother. Can you smell the flowers?"

"We haven't what we need to celebrate Passover," Naomi said grimly.

"I'll go back to Bethlehem and buy whatever we need."

"With what? Will you beg? Will you prostitute yourself?

They won't give you anything. You saw how they looked at you. You know how they acted."

"We have a few coins left."

Naomi glared, her eyes awash with tears. "And what will we do when those run out?"

"The Lord will help us."

"The Lord has forgotten us!" Naomi looked around the cave. "He has forgotten me!" She drew her shawl over her face and wept bitterly.

Ruth pressed trembling lips together until she knew she wouldn't weep along with her. She must be gentle but firm. "We are home, Mother. We are back among your people. God *will* help us. He helped us get here, and He will help us survive." She put her hand on Naomi's knee. "You said we should trust in God and so we shall. You said we should love Him with all our heart, our mind, and our strength. And so we shall." Her voice broke softly. "Now, please tell me. What do we need for Passover?"

Naomi lowered her shawl, her face ravaged by tears. "I can't even remember, Ruth. After the first few years in Moab, Elimelech stopped celebrating the feasts of the Lord. And I couldn't."

Ruth sat beside her and took her hand. She stroked it. "It will come back to you. Tell me about the way it was when you were a little girl."

As Naomi talked, she relaxed and remembered. "We'll need a shank bone from a lamb, bitter herbs, an onion, a candle, and grain. The Feast of Unleavened Bread begins the day after. It will take everything . . ."

"We have enough."

"What will we do when everything is gone?"

"We will live this day alone. God will take care of tomorrow."

Naomi shook her head, weeping. "Where did you learn such faith?"

Ruth smiled at her. "Where else? From you."

Ruth returned to Bethlehem, purchased what they needed with the few coins she had left—the coins that had decorated her wedding headdress—and headed back. On the way through town, she filled the skin with water.

Water was free.

+ + +

The day after Passover, Ruth gave Naomi the last of the parched grain. "I'm going back into Bethlehem to buy some supplies."

"With what? We have nothing."

"I have these." She removed two thin gold bracelets.

"Oh, no. Mahlon gave those to you!"

"As long as I live, I will never forget Mahlon." She kissed Naomi's pale cheek. "Would your son want us to go hungry? Rest now. I'll return as soon as I can."

All through the day, worry plagued Ruth. How would she provide for her mother-in-law when money ran out and she had nothing more to sell? She prayed unceasingly as she walked through the marketplace. *Lord, I don't know what to do. Help me take care of my mother-in-law.* Ruth bargained with four merchants before she got the price that she wanted for her bracelets. Then she bargained even harder for the lowest price for dates, a jar of olive oil, an ephah of parched grain, and an extra blanket for Naomi, who had shivered through the night. Her purchases took everything she had.

She knew that other women in her situation had resorted to prostitution, but she would rather die than bring such shame on herself or Naomi. Would she and her mother-in-law have no recourse but to sit at the city gate each day and beg others for charity? She was young and able-bodied. Perhaps she could sell herself as a slave and give the money to Naomi. But what would happen to Naomi when the twenty shekels ran out? There must be another way.

Lord, what must I do? I will do whatever is in accordance with Your Law for the sake of Your servant, Naomi. But we have only enough to sustain us for a few more days. Show me the way to provide for my mother-in-law and not bring further shame upon her.

When Ruth stopped at the well to refill the skin, she noticed several women decorating their doorways. Though they glanced her way frequently, no one greeted her. Ruth shifted the things she was carrying so she could manage the skin of water and headed back to the cave.

"The women were hanging garlands of greenery," she told Naomi upon her return.

"They're preparing for the Feast of Firstfruits."

"Are there many feasts?" Ruth wondered aloud. Silently, she worried about how she would provide what was needed. *Oh, Lord, Lord, what must I do? I am defeated already.*

"Sit with me awhile, and I'll tell you about the feasts of the Lord," Naomi said.

Ruth sat just inside the mouth of the small cave, where she was sheltered from the sun.

"We've arrived in Bethlehem in time to celebrate four feasts of the Lord," Naomi said. "There are seven each year. We've celebrated Passover and are now beginning the six days of the Feast of the Unleavened Bread. The barley is the first grain crop to be harvested, and it's ready now for reaping, so the women are making preparations for the third feast, the Feast of Firstfruits. Men will be chosen to cut stalks of barley for the procession. The stalks will be brought to the priest, who will present them before the Lord. Fifty days after that, we'll celebrate the fourth feast, the Feast of Weeks, when the wheat harvest begins. We'll bake two loaves of bread with fine flour and leaven to be presented to the Lord by a priest on the high place."

Wheat cost dearly. Ruth looked away, not wanting her mother-in-law to suspect her distress. Naomi mustn't know how bad their situation was. It would only add to her grief.

"There will be three more feasts of the Lord later," Naomi said. "The Feast of Trumpets, the Day of Atonement, and the Feast of Tabernacles." She went on to explain.

Ruth tried to be attentive and absorb everything Naomi was teaching her, but her head was swimming with details, her mind clouded by worries. In fifty days, she and Naomi wouldn't have to worry about how to prepare a feast because they would be starving. She had nothing left to sell, no way of making money, no opportunity to work. There would be no wheat to make bread for the Lord, let alone bread to eat.

"The Law guides our lives," Naomi said. "When we fall away, the Lord disciplines us. As I have been disciplined."

Ruth wanted to cover her face and weep. Instead, she sat silent, gazing outside, hiding her inner turmoil. *Oh, Lord, Lord . . .* She didn't even know how to pray. Perhaps there were special words, ablutions, offerings, *something* that would help her prayer be heard. *Oh, God, have mercy. I want to please You. I want to serve this woman I love who loves You so much. Please, I beseech You. Show me what to do.*

Naomi stretched out her hand. "Do you see this fallow field? Once it was thick with wheat. Elimelech put his hand to the plow and the land prospered. I remember how the wind would blow gently over the stalks so that the field moved in golden waves. We had so much. Life was so good. During those early years, there was so much, Elimelech did not begrudge the gleaners. It wasn't until later that he wouldn't let them come and work, but gathered every stalk, right to the edge of his land." Naomi frowned. "Perhaps that's why . . ."

"Gleaners?" Ruth leaned forward.

Naomi leaned back against the stone. "The Lord commanded that no one reap to the edges or corners of their fields. The grain that grows there is set aside for the poor to gather." She looked out at the field again, troubled and deep in thought. "When all is done according to the ways of the Lord, no one goes hungry."

Ruth closed her eyes in relief and bowed her head. *Oh, Yahweh, You are truly a God of mercy.* Her heart filled with so much gratitude, her throat closed hot with tears. She hadn't realized how afraid she was of the future until this moment when she felt hope surge again. God had not forsaken them! She almost laughed at her ignorance. She had grown up in a city and knew nothing about the ways of farmers. She had grown up in the shadow of Chemosh, a false god who took and never gave back. And now, here was the God who loved His people and provided for them— even the poorest of the poor, the brokenhearted, the broken in spirit.

Truly, Jehovah, You are a merciful redeemer and gracious protector! I should have remembered how You protected us every step of the way from Kir-hareseth over the mountains to Bethlehem. Forgive me, Lord; forgive Your foolish handmaiden. How could I have believed You would bring us so far only to let us starve?

Smiling, Ruth lifted her head and filled her lungs with air, her heart swelling with gratitude and a strange sense of complete freedom.

✦   ✦   ✦

And the women were saying . . .

"Poor Naomi. Do you remember how she used to laugh and be so confident?"

"Too confident, if you ask me."

"Elimelech wasn't the only man who wanted to marry her."

"Do you remember how handsome he was?"

"Naomi is a year younger than I am, and she looks so old."

"And thin."

"Grief does that. A husband and two sons dead. Oy."

"God must be punishing her."

"All she has to show for the years in Moab is that girl who came with her."

"She looks so foreign."

"Such dark eyes."

"You've heard about Moabite women . . ."

"No, what did you hear?"

They clustered together, whispering, gasping, shaking their heads.

"Naomi should send that girl home to Moab where she belongs. We don't want her kind around here."

"Yes, I agree. But who among us will take Naomi in?"

"Well, I can't!"

"I've barely enough to feed my own family."

"I have no room."

"Then what will happen to her?"

"God will take care of her."

+ + +

The day after the Feast of Firstfruits, Ruth rose and asked Naomi for permission to go out into the fields and gather leftover grain.

"Not everyone will welcome you, Ruth," Naomi said, alarmed.

"But the Law allows—"

"Not everyone heeds the Law. My own husband and sons—"

"I must go, Mother. This is the only way."

"But I'm afraid for you. There are men in the fields who will try to take advantage of you. They'll see nothing wrong in assaulting a Moabitess."

"Then I will work alongside the women."

"They'll be no better. I don't know what I'd do if something happened to you."

Ruth embraced and kissed her. "I will pray that the Lord protects me, that He is a shield around me." She smiled into Naomi's frightened eyes. "Perhaps God will lead me to the field of some kind man who will allow me to glean the free grain behind his reapers. Pray for that."

"You must watch out."

"I will."

"Don't turn your back on anyone."

"I'll be careful."

"All right, my daughter, go ahead," Naomi finally relented.

Ruth walked along the road and entered the first field where reapers were at work, but she didn't stay more than a few minutes. Another gleaner hurled a stone. Ruth uttered a cry as it struck her cheek. She stumbled quickly from the field, hearing the woman shouting. "Get out of here, you Moabite harlot! Go back where you belong!" Staunching the trickle of blood on her cheek, Ruth went on. The reapers in the next field were no kinder.

"Moabite whore! Go back to your own kind and stay out of our fields!"

"And stay away from our men!"

When she started to enter another field, the workers leered at her. "Come here, my pretty one!" an overseer called to her. "I'm in need of a roll in the hay." The other men laughed.

Ruth ran back onto the road, her face aflame as the men and women laughed. They continued to call out insults and make jokes about Moabites as she hurried away.

She walked on and on, passing fields of wheat not yet ripe

for harvest. Finally she came to another barley field, where the men were girded and hard at work with their scythes. Women worked behind them, gathering the stalks of barley and bundling them. There were no gleaners. Dejected, Ruth wondered if it was a sign of the owner's attitude toward the destitute. She could only hope the absence of gleaners was due to the field's considerable distance from Bethlehem. She looked around cautiously. Surely the owner had some compassion, for he had erected a shelter where his workers could rest. Some of the men and women in the field sang as they worked.

Swallowing her fear, Ruth approached the overseer standing near the shelter. He was a tall man, a powerfully built man with a solemn demeanor. Clasping her hands and keeping her eyes downcast, she bowed before him. "Greetings, sir."

"What do you want, woman?"

Heart pounding, she straightened and saw how his gaze moved down over her grimly. Would he deny her the right to glean because she was a foreigner? "I've come to ask your permission to pick up the stalks dropped by the reapers." She would beg if necessary.

Frowning, he stood silent, considering her request. Then he nodded and pointed. "There will be more grain for you if you glean at the corners of the field and along the edge."

Relief swept through Ruth. She let out her breath sharply and smiled. "Thank you, sir!" She bowed once more. "Thank you!" He looked so startled, she blushed and lowered her head quickly.

"Stay clear of the workers," he said as she left him.

"Yes, sir." She bowed again. "Thank you for your kindness, sir." She felt him watching her closely as she hurried away. The reapers took notice of her as she hastened toward the farthest corner of the field. One woman gathering the stalks behind the reapers glanced at her and smiled. No one cast an insult or threw a stone. No one called out lewd propositions or insults. The workers in this field left her alone. They kept on with their own work and began to sing again.

Relieved and thankful, Ruth set to work. Without tools, she had to break off the stalks of barley with her bare hands. Soon her fingers were blistered. Hour after hour she worked while the sun beat down hot and heavy. She became light-headed from the heat and labor and sat in the shade of a tree near the boundary stone until she was rested enough to begin work again. *I will be like an ant laying up stores of grain through the spring and summer months so there will be food to last through the winter,* she thought, smiling as she worked. Each hour was important, and she threw herself into the labor, grateful she had been given freedom to do so.

The songs of the reapers lifted her spirits. "The earth is the Lord's in all its fullness . . . maker of heaven and earth . . . ruler of all . . . who delivered us from Pharaoh . . . holy is Your name. . . ."

Ruth hummed as she worked, and when she learned the words, she sang with them.

+ + +

Boaz had checked the work in all of his barley fields but one. He rode his horse along the road, raising his hand in greeting to those he recognized overseeing or working in the fields. Some elders at the gate shook their heads at him, asking why he always felt it necessary to spend so much time in the fields with his workers. His overseers had proven themselves trustworthy. Why not leave the work to them and sit and talk with those of his station? They never understood why he enjoyed being a part of the harvest, and not just showing up for the celebration at the end.

He had worked in his father's fields as a boy when the crops had come in fourfold. And he had worked in the fields as a young man when famine was upon the land. Surely it was through the mercy of God alone that he'd prospered while many others had struggled. Many had sold their land and sought a better life elsewhere. Rather than repent and turn to God again, they had despaired and moved on, necks stiff with pride as they continued to bow down to the baals and Ashtoreth.

Elimelech had left that way. Boaz had tried to reason with him, but the man had never been one to listen, even to a close relative. "What good is the Promised Land when it won't yield grain?" It seemed beyond Elimelech's reasoning to see that God had turned away because His own people had proven themselves unfaithful. "Stop bowing down to the baals and stay here, Elimelech. Think of what is best for your sons. Work your land. Surely the Lord will bless you if you're faithful," Boaz had urged him.

"Faithful? I've given sacrifices. I've given offerings."

"What God wants is a contrite heart."

"Why should I be contrite when I've done everything I was supposed to do? What good has it done me? Here you stand, Boaz, thinking you're a better Jew than I am. All you have over me is better land."

Elimelech never could see his blessings.

Boaz didn't want to think about the past, but it was there stirring long-forgotten feelings inside him, feelings he thought he'd smothered by hard work. But they were like the hyssop that grew from a stone wall. What use was there in going over hard words exchanged twenty years ago? What use in reliving the pain and frustration of trying to help another before he brought disaster on his own head? Elimelech had failed to realize how richly he'd been blessed by God, even during those famine years. Mightily blessed, but blind to see it. Boaz had talked long and hard and succeeded in accomplishing nothing but a broken relationship and hard feelings on his cousin's side. All these years later, Boaz could still remember as though it were this morning when he stood at the city gate watching Elimelech take Naomi and their two sons away from Bethlehem.

Ah, Naomi, sweet, vibrant Naomi . . .

He'd wept that day, though no one had known the fullness of his grief.

Since then, the Lord had poured bounty into his hands, so much bounty that it naturally overflowed into the hands of others in need of it. The long years had been filled with purpose and thanksgiving, if not the joy he had hoped for. He'd always had more than he needed and knew he had God to thank for it. Even though the Lord had denied him the one thing he'd prayed for with such fervent longing, Boaz praised His name. God was sovereign, and it wasn't for a man to question or grieve for what he could not have. Boaz found contentment in accepting his life as it was and thanking God for it.

As he rounded the curve, Boaz saw the field of ripe grain stretching out before him. The workers were singing as they worked. He smiled, for he wanted his servants to be happy in their labor and not just going through the motions to receive what they needed to sustain life. Life should be bounteous, and he did what he could to make it so for those who worked for him. Surely the pleasure men and women received from food and drink and the work of their hands was a gift from the hand of God.

A young woman worked in the farthest corner of his field. He'd never seen her before, but he knew by her dress that she was not from among his people. A Moabite. Most gleaners stayed within easy walking distance of the city. Why had this one come so far? He dismounted and tied up his horse near the shelter. "Good day, Shamash. The work is going well, I see."

"Indeed, Boaz. The crop is even better than last year."

"Who is that girl over there?"

"She is the young woman from Moab who came back with Naomi. She asked me this morning if she could gather grain behind the harvesters. She has been hard at work ever since, except for a few minutes' rest over there in the shelter."

Naomi's daughter-in-law! He had heard about her soon after the two women arrived in Bethlehem. People had been talking about the young Moabitess ever since.

"She has come a long way to glean."

"She looked as though she'd had a hard time at another field."

Boaz glanced at him. "Then she did well to come here." He put his hand on Shamash's arm and smiled. "Talk with the young men, and make sure no one bothers her." He went out into the field among his servants and spoke to them. "The Lord be with you!"

"The Lord bless you!" they said in return.

When he went to the young woman at the corner of the field, she stopped working and bowed her head in respect. She didn't look into his eyes, but she greeted him like a slave would greet a master. She showed uncommon respect. His heart softened when he saw how the stalks of barley in her hand shook slightly. "Listen, my daughter," he said gently. "Stay right here with us when you gather grain; don't go to any other fields. Stay right behind the women working in my field. See which part of the field they are harvesting, and then follow them. I have warned the young men not to bother you. And when you are thirsty, help yourself to the water they have drawn from the well."

She glanced up in surprise. "Thank you." Her smile made her quite beautiful.

He felt an odd sensation in his chest as he looked into her dark eyes. *Here now, what is this?* He felt a twinge of embarrassment at his attraction, for he was more than twice her age.

"Why are you being so kind to me?" she asked, her voice sweet and thickly accented. "I am only a foreigner."

And clearly had been treated as one, for there was a bruise and an abrasion on her cheek. "Yes, I know. But I also know about the love and kindness you have shown your mother-in-law since the death of your husband." His voice deepened as his emotions rose. "I have heard how you left your father and mother and your own land to live here among complete strangers. May the Lord, the God of Israel, under whose wings you have come to take refuge, reward you fully." Surely the Lord had shown great mercy to those who belonged to Him. As Naomi always had. And now, this young woman.

Ruth's cheeks turned red. "I hope I continue to please you, sir," she replied. "You have comforted me by speaking so kindly to me, even though I am not as worthy as your workers."

Noticing the bruise again, he asked gently, "Did someone hit you?"

She frowned slightly and then looked startled. She raised her hand instinctively to cover the mark and lowered her head as though to hide it. "Only a small stone. No great harm done. I suppose it's to be expected."

As though that would excuse such treatment. "It had better not happen in *my* field," he said darkly.

"Oh, it didn't happen here," she said quickly. "No one has bothered me since I arrived."

Boaz felt shame that any of his neighbors would treat her so cruelly.

He wanted her to feel safe, but he didn't want her to misinterpret his intentions. She was a comely young woman, and no doubt had received the attentions of much younger men than he. "Be at ease among us, Ruth. You're safe here."

He left her to her work, thinking as he walked away that young Mahlon had shown uncommon wisdom in choosing a girl like this one to be his wife. Not all foreign women were a curse on Hebrew men, drawing them away from the true

God into lustful pagan worship. Some foreign women had been grafted in among God's chosen people because of their great faith.

His mother, Rahab, had been such a woman. She'd welcomed two Hebrew spies into her house in the wall of Jericho. Unashamed, she had boldly declared to them her faith in Yahweh, the God of the Hebrews. She'd risked her life to be aligned with God and His people. One of those spies had been his father, Salmon. And God had blessed both his parents, for they had loved one another throughout their lives.

Nevertheless, God had warned His people against the miseries of yoking themselves to foreigners. Men were too easily seduced away from God by the wiles of women. But what constituted a foreigner? Surely this young Moabitess was one of God's people. She had declared her faith by turning her back on life in Moab and coming to Bethlehem with Naomi. This girl was like his mother, who had been a standing stone of faith among a mountain of loose gravel. Boaz often wondered if it wasn't faith—not just Hebrew blood— that declared one chosen by God. For surely it was and always had been God who selected those who would belong to Him.

But perhaps that was merely the old hurt rising within Boaz, rationalizing and justifying the match his father had made. Even after all these years, he felt the pang of rejection. Hadn't he been turned away as a suitor because he was half Canaanite? There were those among God's people who thought the bloodline to Abraham was all that God counted as righteous, and faith a mere by-product of blood.

Boaz paused at the edge of his field, gazing back at the young woman gleaning behind his reapers. She gathered a stalk here and a stalk there, cradling them in her arms. Her attire proclaimed her a young woman of the city. Yet, here she was in his field, doing backbreaking work in the heat of the day, and grateful for the opportunity. And why did she work so hard? To provide for her Hebrew mother-in-law. Were there any young women among his people that would do such a thing for someone not of Abraham's blood?

Something stirred within him, pain and pleasure at the same time. How long since he had felt this yearning? He smiled in self-mockery and turned away.

A pity Ruth was so young, and he so old.

✦   ✦   ✦

Ruth heard a man call her name. When she glanced up, she saw Boaz standing before the shelter, motioning for her to come. "Come over here and help yourself to some of our food. You can dip your bread in the wine if you like."

Her heart thumped heavily as she placed her gleanings in a careful bundle and left them where she had been working. She was amazed that a man of his station would take notice of a dirty, sweating foreigner at all, let alone invite her to share a meal with his workers. Before entering the shelter, she washed her hands in the water provided. She was embarrassed by the curious looks of his workers. The men perused her from the hem of her dress to the top of her head, while the women whispered among themselves.

"May I sit here?" she said at an open place among his maidservants.

The girl sitting closest moved over. "Should I say no when the master has invited you?"

Ruth's face went hot. When she sat down, she noticed how the girl beside her shifted again, increasing the distance between them. Folding her hands in her lap, she bowed her head and closed her eyes as Boaz blessed the food. When he finished, those around her began to talk among themselves again. They made no effort to include her in their conversation, nor did she expect it of them. She was surprised to see the master himself serving his workers. When Boaz came to her, he gave her a double portion. She glanced up in surprise and saw him frowning down at her hands. She drew them back and clasped them beneath the table again. Had she committed some breach of etiquette? When she dared look up, the others glanced away, talking among themselves. She was so hungry her stomach rumbled loudly, embarrassing her even more. Boaz had given her more than enough to satisfy her hunger. She put half of the double portion of bread into her shawl for Naomi, and then tore off a piece of the second portion and dipped it into the wine.

Gradually, the whispering curiosity lessened as the young women around her talked and laughed, as did the young men on the other side of the enclosure.

Ruth watched Boaz surreptitiously as he sat with his overseer. Despite the disparity of their positions, the two men talked with the ease of good friends. The overseer was young enough to be Boaz's son. He was a handsome man, powerfully built with dark hair and eyes. Boaz was plain. His hair and beard were streaked with gray, the two thick curls at his temples white. He was not attractive in any way that would draw attention. Yet his kindness made her heart soften toward him. His tender care touched some deep place within her. When he turned his head slightly and looked her way, she lowered her eyes again. It was not proper for her to study any man, let alone one who was so far above her station. As she looked away, she encountered the open stares of several young men. One grinned at her. She looked away quickly so that he would know his attentions were unwelcome.

She did not linger over the meal but returned quickly to the field, gleaning in the distant corner where she would neither offend the maidservants nor attract unwanted interest from the reapers.

+ + +

Boaz took Shamash aside before the reapers returned to the fields. "The young men have taken notice of the Moabitess."

He laughed softly. "Any man breathing would take notice of her."

"See that no one takes advantage of her."

Shamash's grin faded. "Of course." He nodded.

Boaz put his hand on the overseer's arm. "I know you wouldn't allow her to be mistreated, but there are those, even among our workers, who are clearly disturbed by the presence of a Moabitess."

"The young women." His mouth tipped.

Boaz removed his hand from Shamash. "Did you notice her fingers are raw and bleeding?"

Frowning, Shamash looked out into the field where Ruth was working. "She hasn't the tools for the work."

"Precisely. When I've gone, go out and tell her to glean behind the workers. Give this young woman time and opportunity to prove herself."

Then Boaz called the younger men to him. When they gathered around him, he looked each in the eye. "You have all noticed the young gleaner among us. Her name is Ruth, and she's providing for her mother-in-law, Naomi, wife of our brother Elimelech. Let her gather grain right among the sheaves without stopping her. And pull out some heads of barley from the bundles and drop them on purpose for her. Let her pick them up, and don't give her a hard time! Whatsoever you do to this young woman, you do to me."

Thus advised, the reapers returned to the field. Boaz mounted his horse.

"Be at ease about the young Moabitess, Boaz," Shamash said. "Everything will be carried out according to your will."

Boaz looked out over his field and the reapers and harvesters cutting and gathering the sheaves. He loved those who belonged to him, and he wanted them to behave with honor toward those less fortunate. Ruth worked alone. "Perhaps God will shine His countenance upon her and give her a young husband from among our people." He looked down at Shamash and smiled. "May God be with you, my friend."

Shamash smiled. "And with you, my lord."

As Boaz rode away, he kept his eyes straight ahead on the road back to Bethlehem, refusing himself the pleasure of looking back at the young Moabitess working in his field. Instead, he thanked God for giving him the opportunity to help her, and thus help another who mattered greatly to him.

Sweet, vibrant Naomi, the girl he had once sought for his wife.

✦   ✦   ✦

Ruth straightened and watched Boaz ride away. "Lord, please bless this man for his kindness toward me and my mother-in-law. Give him joy in his old age." Smiling, she bent to glean again.

The overseer came out to her. She paused in her labor and inclined her head in respect. "I'm to give you instructions from Boaz," he said. "You are to glean among the workers. They won't bother you."

She looked off toward the road down which Boaz had ridden. "I've never known anyone so kind."

"There are few like Boaz." His mouth tipped ruefully. "The Lord brought you to his field. And may the Lord continue to watch over you." He nodded toward the other workers. "Go and join them."

The women sang as they worked. "The Lord is my strength, my song, and my salvation. He is my God, and I will praise Him. He is my father's God—I will exalt Him. The Lord is a warrior—yes, Jehovah is His name. . . ." Ruth quickly absorbed the words and began to sing with them. They glanced at her in surprise. Several smiled. One made a point of snapping off the heads of barley and dropping them for her. Ruth put her palms together and nodded deeply in gratitude.

She worked until evening and then beat out the barley. She had a half bushel of grain! "Surely it is You, Lord, who has provided so much." Filled with a sense of joy and satisfaction, she tied the corners of her shawl and lifted the grain to her back, heading home toward the city of Bethlehem and the small cave where Naomi waited.

✦ ✦ ✦

And the men were saying . . .

"That's the first time I've ever known Boaz to take such interest in a gleaner."

"He's always been kind to gleaners."

"It took courage for her to come out here."

"It looked to me like she may have tried some other fields. Did you see the bruise on her face?"

"Did you know she's gleaning for one of our own widows?"

"No."

"There are probably a lot of people who don't know why she's here."

"And that's an excuse for throwing rocks at her? The Law is clear about gleaners."

"And clear about foreign women."

"Boaz's mother was a foreign woman."

"I suggest we concentrate on our work and mind our own business."

✦ ✦ ✦

And the women were saying . . .

"Do you see how the men are cutting stalks and tossing them over to her?"

"When a girl is pretty, men turn helpful."

"Boaz spoke to them before he left. He probably told them to give her extra grain."

"So even the master is interested in her. Look there. Do you see?"

"See what?"

"Shimei is looking at her again."

"Well, if you weren't staring at Shimei, you wouldn't know that."

"I don't like her."

"Why?"

"Do I have to have a reason?"

"Well, I like her."

"Why?"

"Unlike some I know, the girl works hard and minds her own business."

✦   ✦   ✦

"So much!" Naomi exclaimed, rising as Ruth entered their dwelling place and lowered the bundle of grain from her back. The girl was smiling brightly, her eyes aglow. "Where did you gather all this grain today? May the Lord bless the one who helped you!"

"I've been saying prayers of thanksgiving for the man all the way home, Naomi. His field is some distance from the city."

Naomi didn't ask why Ruth had ventured so far, seeing the bruise on her cheek. She was afraid she knew the answer. "What was the landowner's name?"

"The man I worked with today is named Boaz."

Naomi put her hand to her throat. "Boaz?"

"Yes, Boaz." Ruth took the bread she had saved and handed it to Naomi. "He invited me into the shelter where his maid-servants and reapers ate the midday meal, and gave me a double portion!" She held out a piece of bread. "I've never heard of a man in his position stooping to serve his workers."

Naomi took the bread with trembling fingers. She hadn't given a thought to Boaz when she returned to Bethlehem. She had forgotten all about him. Or maybe the truth was that she had deliberately put the man out of her mind. Just thinking about him made her cringe with shame. Many years ago, he had come to her father and made an offer of marriage for her. How she had carried on as soon as he left the house! How she'd wept and pleaded that her father accept Elimelech instead.

"But he hasn't even offered for you!" her father had said, red-faced with anger.

"He will. His sister told me he has spoken to his father about it."

"Boaz is a man of unquestioned virtue, my daughter."

Indeed, but he was not a man to make a girl's heart beat with love. She wanted a tall husband, ruddy and handsome with laughing eyes and winning ways. She wanted Elimelech. His name meant "my god, a king." Surely that was an indication of his character. The love she saw in Boaz's eyes had embarrassed her. She had been impatient with his attention, repulsed by it. Why wouldn't he go away? Why wouldn't he look for some other girl, one as plain as he?

She had known none of those reasons would sway her father against Boaz, but one thing would—a fact he seemed to have forgotten. "Boaz has unquestioned virtue, Father, but questionable blood." His mother was Canaanite. And a prostitute.

Naomi lowered her head and closed her eyes tightly. *Oh,*

Lord God, that Boaz of all men should be so kind! What shallowness she had shown toward this man. And to look down upon his mother, who had proven herself a woman of such strong faith! Unthinkable! Unpardonable! Yet, despite Naomi's sins against him, Boaz welcomed Ruth and poured a double blessing out for her. "Praise the Lord for a man like that! May the Lord bless him!" she said, her words choked with tears. She deserved his condemnation but received his compassion. She hadn't recognized his worth when she was young, but life had taught her hard lessons. She was older now and far wiser.

A tiny spark of hope came to life within her.

Raising her head slowly, she looked at Ruth. "He is showing his kindness to us as well as to your dead husband." She saw confusion in the girl's eyes. There were so many things yet to teach her about Hebrew ways and the Law. What would be her response if she were to tell Ruth the fullness of Boaz's obligations to them? Would Ruth respond the same way she herself had all those years ago, seeing only the outer shell of the man and not his lion heart? She had never known a man to be more bent upon pleasing God than Boaz. Sadly, a young woman's heart was not often won by a man's character.

"That man is one of our closest relatives, one of our family redeemers, Ruth."

"No wonder he was so kind to me."

"No," she said quickly, not wanting her daughter-in-law to misunderstand. "Boaz is not the sort of man to limit his kindness to family members, Ruth. He has always been kind to anyone in need."

"Even foreigners?"

"His mother was a Canaanite. In fact, she was a prostitute who lived in the wall of Jericho." When Ruth's eyes widened, Naomi hastened to explain. "She was a woman of great faith, but there were many people who looked down upon Boaz when he was a young man because he was of mixed blood. Hebrew on his father's side, and Canaanite on his mother's. Rahab hid two spies sent out by Joshua before our people took the land promised us by God. She declared her faith in Yahweh and saved the men's lives by letting them down from her window by a rope. They went back for her and brought her out when the city was being destroyed, and she lived among our people from that time on. One of the spies took Rahab as his wife."

"Then perhaps Boaz was kind to me for his mother's sake."

Naomi was certain that was not the only reason. "He would understand better than anyone that God calls whom He chooses." If God had called Rahab to be of His own people, then He could call a young Moabite widow as well. She leaned forward. "Did he say anything else to you?" Had Boaz mentioned her?

"Boaz even told me to come back and stay with his harvesters until the entire harvest is completed."

Naomi felt a rush of relief. Surely Boaz wouldn't have encouraged Ruth if he held the ill will of a long-ago rejected suitor. "This is wonderful! Do as he said, Ruth. Stay with his workers right through the whole harvest. You will be safe there, unlike in other fields."

As she ate the bread Boaz had given Ruth, Naomi smiled to herself. She watched her daughter-in-law pour the barley into a basket, careful not to lose a single seed of grain. It seemed all was not lost after all. There was one door left to open so that Ruth could walk through into a future and a hope. And, if God was willing, the door would stay open for her as well.

+ + +

Naomi awakened when she heard a soft cascading of rocks just outside the cave. The sun was barely up and Ruth was coming up the slope, carrying a large skin of water. "You're awake early," Ruth said, smiling.

"I thought I would go into Bethlehem today and talk with some of my old friends."

Ruth poured the water from the skin into a large earthen jug. "Good. I'm sure they've missed you and will have plenty to talk about with you." She hung up the empty skin and swung her black shawl over her hair and shoulders. "I'll try to be back before dark."

"God be with you, Ruth."

Ruth smiled brightly. "And with you, Mother."

Naomi rose. Dragging a blanket around her shoulders, she went to the mouth of the cave and watched Ruth head down the road. Naomi stood amazed that God had blessed her with such a daughter-in-law. Ruth had left behind opportunities and possibilities. She had turned away from a secure future in Kir-hareseth so that she could come here to Bethlehem and live in this cave with a tired, despairing, complaining old woman. At any time, her daughter-in-law could have returned to the home of her affluent parents, but instead she went off every morning to do the work of the poorest of the poor. Not once had she uttered a word of complaint. Every evening, she returned with a smile, grain, glad tidings, and a grateful heart.

A man of discernment like Boaz would appreciate a young woman with Ruth's virtues, Moabitess or not.

Naomi drew herself up before she allowed her thoughts to run rampant. It wouldn't do to make plans for Ruth's future before learning the facts. Naomi had no intention of rushing into Bethlehem, seeking out the elders, and making a case. No, she would move slowly. There was no hurry, now that she and Ruth had shelter and food. She would take time to observe, take time to let people get to know her daughter-in-law . . . for who could not respect her when they did? Was there a finer young woman than her precious Ruth? Above all, Naomi would take time to pray for God's guidance, even though it was surely God Himself who had planted this seed of hope in her mind.

For the first time since burying her last son, Naomi saw what life could hold in the future instead of what life had held in the past.

✦ ✦ ✦

And the women were saying . . .

"I think she's pretty."

"That's because you like her."

"You're just jealous because Rimon, Netzer, and Tirosh were trying to talk with her today."

"Have you noticed how she never works near the men?"

"She never even gives them a second glance."

"She must have loved Mahlon very much."

"She's certainly loyal to her mother-in-law."

"My mother said Ruth comes to the well early every

morning and takes water back to her mother-in-law before she comes to the fields."

"Then she must be up well before dawn."

"Shamash keeps an eye on her."

"So do all the men!"

"No one's going to marry a Moabitess who's already had a husband."

"I would be sorry to see Ruth and her mother-in-law live out their days in that cave."

"They live in a cave?"

"The one just below town where the shepherds keep their flocks in the winter. Didn't you know?"

"I thought they lived in the city."

"Naomi spends her time in the city, visiting with friends and bartering."

"What about the house that belonged to her husband?"

"I heard my father say Naomi's husband mortgaged it and all his land before taking the family to Moab."

"Everybody is talking about them."

"Especially about Ruth, I would imagine."

"You're jealous!"

"I'm not jealous!"

"Then why do you dislike her so much?"

"Foreign women rouse the worst kind of interest in our men."

"Foreign women don't make a habit of going to the synagogue."

"Now you're telling me she's a proselyte?"

"Ruth attends every Sabbath with her mother-in-law, drinking in every word the priest reads from the Law. They stand at the back with the other widows. That's probably why you haven't noticed them. You're up front near the screen where you can look through and see Netzer."

"How you talk, Tirzah, when you're no better, gawking at Lahad all day."

"Can I help myself? He's so handsome."

The young women entered Bethlehem laughing together.

+ + +

"He's not married?" Naomi said in surprise, feeling a pang of guilt at this bit of information given to her by Sigal, a friend from years past. "What's wrong with the man that he's not taken a wife by this age?"

"Nothing." Sigal poured grains of wheat onto the grinding stone. "He probably never had time to seek a wife. He's poured his life into building up his estate. Boaz isn't like other landowners. He's out there in the fields every day. And when he's not, he's at the city gate helping settle disputes."

"What good is an estate without sons to inherit?"

"He's not in the grave yet, Naomi. He can still look for a wife, if he has a mind to do so. Believe me, there are plenty of fathers who would throw their daughters at Boaz if he broached the subject of marriage. He's become the wealthiest man in Bethlehem."

"And probably the loneliest."

Sigal gave a snort of laughter. "The man has no time to be lonely."

"Still, it's a pity he isn't married."

"Maybe he's waiting for the perfect woman, someone beautiful and intelligent and who has the faith of his mother. Some men have expectations so high they can never be met."

"Some men want a wife who will love them."

"Boaz is loved and respected by everyone in Bethlehem."

"I mean he might be waiting for someone to fall in love with him."

"I doubt that. Most men know love takes time. As long as the girl respects her husband, there's every reason to hope for a happy marriage."

"You are a wise woman, Sigal."

"I always was."

Naomi couldn't help wondering. Had she hurt Boaz so badly he never dared ask another woman to marry him? She felt grieved at that thought. Surely that wasn't the reason he had remained without a wife. Boaz was too sensible to give up marriage just because of one foolish girl.

Should she ask him about it?

Her heart lurched. No! Never! She couldn't say a word about the past without embarrassing Boaz and possibly jeopardizing the future. She wanted to make up for the pain she had caused him so many years ago. Whatever his reasons for not taking a wife, it made her sad to think of him living out his life alone. A man was not meant to be alone. And certainly not a man like Boaz. God had blessed him with land and possessions, but surely it was a sign that He had not blessed the man with the one thing he needed to fulfill his life: a wife who would bear him sons. The man should have a family of his own.

"I remember a rumor I heard years ago," Sigal said, continuing to grind wheat. "About you and Boaz." She gave Naomi a teasing smile.

"Rumors aren't worth the sand we walk on," Naomi said.

If the rumor was revived, it would only serve to humiliate a good man. "Elimelech paid my father the bride-price when I was fourteen."

"All the young women were envious of you. Elimelech was very handsome."

"Were they envious of me when he mortgaged the land and took me and our young sons away from Bethlehem?"

Sigal blinked in surprise.

Naomi grimaced at her own harshness. "I'm sorry, my friend. Even after all these years, I still remember the bitterness of that day."

Sigal stopped her grinding and placed her hand over Naomi's. "I thought of you many times over the years."

Tears filled Naomi's eyes. "I longed for home every day I was gone." She drew in her breath and released a contented sigh. "But for all that, the Lord blessed me with Ruth."

"Truly," Sigal said. "She loves you as though you were her own mother."

"I could not love her more if she were from my own flesh."

"God has comforted you through her, Naomi. Everyone says she is a young woman of excellence."

Naomi was pleased. Ruth was no longer looked upon as "the Moabitess." Surely the Lord Himself had seen that her virtues had not gone unnoticed by those who dwelt in Bethlehem.

The question remained: Had Boaz noticed?

four

BOAZ came by the barley field every day to see how
the work progressed. And every day, he took cautious
notice of the young Moabitess working close behind his
reapers. He didn't speak to her, concerned that his attentions might cause his workers to gossip. When he stayed to
share a meal with his workers, he made sure he kept his gaze
away from the young woman. Never had he found anything
more difficult to do!

The barley harvest was over, and the wheat stood tall and
ripe, ready for the reapers. In another few weeks, all the
grain would be harvested. Had Ruth gleaned enough to
carry herself and Naomi through the year? He knew they
lived in the cave within the boundaries of Bethlehem.
Elimelech had owned the field near it. But did they have
enough stored to carry them through until next harvest?

Boaz looked out at the workers. "Has the young Moabitess made any friends among our people?" he asked his overseer.

"All of them look upon her with respect and admiration."

That was not what he'd asked, but Boaz understood the implication. Ruth was admired from a distance, much as his mother had been.

"What about the young men? Has she taken interest in anyone in particular?"

"She never leaves the company of the maidservants. She pays no attention to the men. Unlike some of our other young women, I've never seen Ruth do anything to draw attention to herself. She comes early to the field and works late. And she seems content with the work. I hear her singing with the maidservants." Shamash smiled. "She always asks me to extend her thanks to you. Is there a reason you don't speak with her yourself?"

"You know how people talk." Boaz mounted his horse. "You like her, don't you, Shamash?"

"Everyone admires her, Boaz. I've never known a young woman more worthy of praise. I haven't heard a word said against her, even in the city." Shamash looked out at the young woman working in the field. "She would make a good wife."

Boaz felt a pang of discomfort. Was Shamash falling in love with Ruth? Boaz didn't like the sinking feeling in his stomach. Should he begrudge another man happiness? Who knew better than he that a man alone was often lonely, even among friends. "A good wife is worth more than her weight in gold, Shamash. She is a crown on her husband's head. The young woman out there would bring honor to any man." He saw Ruth look up and averted his gaze. He was startled to find Shamash staring at him with an odd smile. Frowning slightly, Boaz gave a nod. "May the Lord bless you in your endeavors, Shamash."

Shamash bowed. "And may the Lord grant you your heart's desire, Boaz."

It was a long ride back to Bethlehem. Boaz gave charge of his horse to a waiting servant and talked with the elders at the gate. He was occupied with various disputes and business affairs of the city until he saw the maidservants returning to the city. His pulse quickened when he saw Ruth among them. She was walking along the road with his girls, listening and smiling over their carefree chatter, but not joining in. He was startled when he saw Naomi pass by. She went out the gate to meet her daughter-in-law. They kissed one another in greeting and talked briefly as the other young women walked through the gate into Bethlehem. When Ruth and Naomi turned toward their humble home, Ruth glanced his way. She smiled and bowed her head respectfully. Naomi was looking at him. He looked away from the two women and forced himself to listen to the elders. What fine point of the Law had they been discussing? Closing his eyes for a moment, he pretended to be deep in thought, when in truth, he was trying to calm the wild gallop of his heart.

+ + +

Naomi studied Ruth's manner each day when she returned home from gleaning in Boaz's fields. She relished every detail Ruth told her about her time with the maidservants and reapers, and she was hungry to hear her every thought about Boaz. But Ruth said nothing about the landowner. She talked about the work and the pleasant maidservants. Sometimes she sang the songs she'd learned while working among them.

But now, Naomi had cause for hope. Today she had stood just inside the gate waiting for Ruth. Boaz hadn't noticed her there, but she had been in a good position to watch the man. Oh, how his head had come up as his maidservants returned. She knew the moment he spotted Ruth.

"Does Boaz come often to the field?"

"He came four times this week and three times the week before that."

Oh! Naomi thought with deepening satisfaction. *The girl keeps count of the landowner's visits!* That was a good sign. "Does he speak with you each time?"

Ruth shook her head. "He hasn't spoken with me since the first day when he gave me permission to glean. He's a very busy man."

"Ha. Not so busy he couldn't show you a little courtesy." She watched Ruth closely to see her reaction to such talk and was satisfied when Ruth protested.

"Oh, Mother, no. Boaz has shown me courtesy beyond measure. Was it not Boaz who made my work easy by telling his reapers to drop grain for me to glean? We're both indebted to him for his kindness. Every grain of barley and wheat we have is due to his kindness."

"You like him?"

Ruth lowered her eyes. "No more than all those who work in his fields." She sat at the mouth of their cave, gazing out at Elimelech's fallow field. "I wonder why he never married,

Mother. How is it God has blessed this man with such pros-
perity but not given him a wife and sons?"

Naomi smiled to herself. Ruth saw past the plainness of
the man to the lion's heart of faith that beat in his breast.
Why not test her a little more and see if her compassion
could not be refined into tenderness of another kind?
"There was never anything in his appearance to commend
him." When Ruth glanced back in surprise, Naomi hastened
on. "A pity he is so homely."

"He's not handsome the way Mahlon was, but I don't
think he's homely."

"Did you find him the least attractive when you first saw
him?"

Ruth blushed. "I never considered . . ." She shook her
head. "Surely you're not saying you think Boaz ugly."

"Would I call a man ugly who puts grain in my hands?
May it never be! But I won't pretend to be blind either. Boaz
is a good man, a man who lives the Law and doesn't just
preach it. But he's wanting in the assets that would win a
girl's heart."

"He has dignity and character."

"Was it dignity and character that made you fall in love
with my son? If Mahlon had been plain, short, and thin,
would you have been attracted to him?"

"Mahlon was more than a handsome face, Mother. You
know that as well as I."

"We aren't talking about love growing in the bonds of
marriage, my dear. We're talking about what you thought
the first time you saw Mahlon striding along the streets of
Kir-hareseth. God was merciful to my son. At least Mahlon

knew the love of a good wife." She shook her head. "Poor Boaz." She clucked her tongue. "He has no one, and it's too late now."

Ruth looked troubled. "Why should it be too late?"

"He's old."

"Oh, Naomi!" Ruth laughed. "You were telling me yesterday that Abraham fathered Isaac when he was one hundred years old, and Boaz can't be more than half that age."

What a jewel Mahlon had received in this girl. If only Mahlon had given her a son, Naomi would not have so many worries. As it stood now, Mahlon's name and the name of Elimelech would die out. Naomi couldn't sit by and let it be so.

Oh, Elimelech, had you been stronger in faith, your sons would be gathering in the wheat from that field down there. You would be enjoying the inheritance God gave you. You would have claimed the promises and lived by the Law and been blessed like Boaz. Instead, my beloved husband, you took us away from our inheritance and gave your life to dreams of wealth. And everything you worked so hard to gain for yourself is gone, used up, blown away like dust. Your life was as fruitless as that fallow field out there. There's nothing to show for all the work you did. Even the fruit of your loins has died. You left nothing behind that will last.

And I'm angry, so angry with you, Elimelech. My very blood cries out against you for wasting our lives. I'm angry with myself because I was so easily swayed by your handsome face, your winning ways, your sweet words that went down and turned sour. You'll never know the full extent of the pain you caused because you wanted to take the easier road rather than the right one.

But as God has forgiven me for my sins and brought me home, I forgive you, too. Because I loved you to the end, no matter the manner of man you were. And besides, you suffered more than anyone for the choices you made.

As much as Naomi had loved her husband, she knew better than anyone that Elimelech had never been the man Boaz was. Her husband had rejected the promises of God, left his land, brought up his sons in a foreign country. When Elimelech had died in Moab, he'd left his family stranded there. His two sons, the fruit of his loins, had taken foreign wives and died in Moab. Through eyes of love, Naomi could see the truth. Elimelech had sinned against God, cast blame on Him for the consequences, and looked out for himself rather than repent. Her husband had believed he could prosper by his own power.

Oh, the foolishness of man.

Boaz was the other side of the coin. He'd chosen to stay in Bethlehem during the hard years when God was punishing His stiff-necked people for bowing down to the baals. He'd claimed the promises of God and lived an upright life before the Lord. And God had blessed him for his steady, stubborn faith. Boaz was wealthy now, a man of high standing in Bethlehem. He sat at the city gate with the elders and made decisions that affected the entire city. Yet he hadn't become puffed up with pride because of his exalted position. Humility was his mantle. He looked out for others less fortunate, even a young widow from Moab.

The cry of Elimelech had always been "God has abandoned us, so *I* will provide!" Boaz's life made his declaration: "God is my provider, and I will trust in Him."

Surely the wife of such a man would have cause for rejoicing. Naomi wanted Ruth to be happy. She wanted this precious girl, who had given up everything to take care of an aging mother-in-law, to have *joy!*

But there was a problem.

Boaz was not the only relative left. Naomi had learned during her visits in town that there was another man more closely related to her than Boaz. A younger man that made the women roll their eyes and smile.

A man like Elimelech.

✦   ✦   ✦

Ruth was disturbed by what Naomi had said about Boaz. When he came to the field the next day, she watched him surreptitiously and felt a strange tenderness for him. Everyone respected him and had great affection for him, but it was the kind they would have for a father or an older brother.

Had any woman ever looked upon Boaz with love? Had the mere sight of him walking by stirred any woman's heart with passion the way hers had been stirred for Mahlon? She couldn't imagine it, and that saddened her. How old was Boaz? Fifty? Sixty?

The poor man. For all his wealth, what did he have that would last?

Oh, Lord, God of Israel, don't let the name of Boaz die out.

She watched him talking with Shamash and thought he looked so solemn. Did he ever laugh? What did he do when he wasn't checking on the progress in his fields, seeing that his servants were well cared for, or serving the community by making heavy decisions at the gate? He had friends, but could he confide in them as he would a woman who loved him? What were his dreams? She had seen the sorrow in his eyes. Was it a sorrow born of having no one who cared enough to look beneath the rugged casing of the man into his heart and spirit?

He must have sensed her attention, for he glanced her way. Her feelings of tenderness swelled, and she smiled, giving him a nod of respect, and quickly looked down. She had cause to be thankful that God had led her to this field and this man. When she glanced up, sensing his perusal, Boaz looked away. One of the maidservants noticed the silent exchange and gave her a curious look. When she spoke to another close by, Ruth felt the heat climb into her cheeks. Did these young women think she was showing an inappropriate interest in their master? He was a rich man, after all. There were women who would want to be his wife for that reason alone, without thought to his feelings.

Shaken, Ruth kept her attention on her work for the rest of the day. She didn't want her interest in Boaz to be misinterpreted. Gossip could destroy her reputation and cause him embarrassment. She would keep her eyes off the man and pray for him instead.

Oh, Lord, God of mercy, remember this man for his kindness toward the less fortunate. Let his name be held in esteem not for this generation only, but for generations to come, for surely Boaz is Your faithful servant. He proclaims Your name with every opportunity. He is a man who desires to please and obey You. Oh, Jehovah-jireh, this lonely man has been a tool of Your mercy and provision. I know You are enough, but surely a man such as this one was not meant to be alone. May it please You to give him whatever his heart desires. . . . Oh, Lord, oh, Lord . . .

She prayed unceasingly for her benefactor. She thought of little else but Boaz while she worked in his field.

And the more she prayed for him and thought about him, the more she saw his goodness.

✦   ✦   ✦

Naomi prayed fervently as well. She set her grief aside in favor of her love for Ruth and a desire to see her daughter-in-law settled somewhere better than in this cave. Naomi knew it was time she stopped grieving and started to live again, no matter how painful the effort. It was time to take a good hard look at her own life instead of attending Elimelech's mistakes. Nothing she supposed would happen had happened. Hadn't she left Kir-hareseth expecting to travel back to Bethlehem alone? And Ruth had come with her. Hadn't she expected to be destitute? And Ruth worked in the fields to sustain her. Hadn't she expected all her friends and family to be dead or gone away? And she'd found half a dozen women she'd known and Boaz, as well as another relative.

Boaz was attracted to Ruth. Anyone who bothered to study the man would know. Naomi also knew him well enough to realize he wouldn't speak up and make any attempts to win her. The man's hair would go white and fall out entirely before he allowed his feelings to show openly.

And Ruth would go on dedicating her life to providing for her poor old mother-in-law. She would work until her back was bent and her womb dry. She'd slave away until Naomi had gone the way of her ancestors. Then what would happen to the poor girl? Should Naomi sit by and watch Ruth dedicate her life to gleaning rather than running a household and raising up children for the Lord? Should she do nothing about Ruth's future? Wasn't it a mother's place to stoke the fires a little? Who else but her and God would care about the future of this precious young woman?

So, Lord, what are we going to do about her? How do we shake up that quiet old man and get his blood moving again? If we wait on him, what chance is there?

Supposing she did think up a plan that would turn Boaz's head. Would Ruth agree to carry it through—whatever it was? Ruth would have to agree!

Naomi spent the next days and nights thinking about Ruth's future and what a good husband Boaz would make. Toward the end of the wheat harvest, she thought of a plan so bold it was certain to capture Boaz's attention. Just imagining his reaction made Naomi laugh. But would Ruth trust her judgment? Would her daughter-in-law heed the advice of an old woman who'd made so many mistakes it might seem a way of life?

In the confusion of her feelings, Naomi could not be sure about her motives. She knew only that the Lord could sort it all out and make things right. She loved Ruth as she would a daughter of her own womb and wanted to see her happily settled, but she also wanted a grandson to claim Mahlon's inheritance and carry on his name. She wanted to make amends to Boaz for the pain she had caused him when she was a young girl. And what better way to do that than by offering him a beautiful young wife with many years of childbearing ahead of her?

Was it right to ask so much of God when she'd spent most of her life walking behind Elimelech?

Ruth and Boaz. Boaz and Ruth. Don't You think they're right for each other, Lord? I grant she is much younger than he, but what better blessing to give a righteous man like Boaz than a quiver full of children in his old age? And what children they would have! You would not see their sons and daughters bowing down to baals!

She pleaded their case to the Almighty and longed for an answer. How fortunate Moses had been to hear The Voice from a burning bush. Naomi knew better than to expect God to give her an audible answer, but she couldn't trust any of her friends with the questions tormenting her. Was this plan right before God? If it wasn't, what might be the cost to Ruth?

Let the cost be on my head, Lord.

✦   ✦   ✦

When the harvest came to an end, Naomi knew the plan had to be put into action now or never. Boaz had been given plenty of time to notice Ruth's virtues, and Ruth had great respect for him.

"My daughter, it's time that I found a permanent home for you, so that you will be provided for. I intend to find a husband for you and get you happily married again."

Ruth laughed. "And who would marry someone like me?"

"The man I'm thinking of is Boaz."

"Boaz!" Ruth spilled some of the grain she was pouring into an earthen container and stared at her. "You can't be serious!"

"I know he's old . . ."

"He's not *old*."

"Homely, then. Is that why you object?"

"Mother, he's the most respected man in all Bethlehem! He stands among the elders at the gate! He's a rich man with land and servants!"

"All the more reason to consider him."

Ruth shook her head, half in amusement, half in consternation. "I know you love me, Mother, but your esteem for the widow of your son is beyond bounds. How can you possibly think I would be worthy of Boaz? The idea is ludicrous."

"You were good enough for my son. You're good enough for Boaz."

Ruth went back to pouring grain into the earthen container. "Not even if I threw myself at his feet would the man notice me."

"You don't think he's noticed you? Ha. He noticed you long ago."

"In kindness."

"More than in kindness. Have you no eyes in your head? He admires you. From too much a distance, but admire you he does."

"You're mistaken. He thinks no more of me than he does any other gleaner in his fields."

"I've made it my business to study the man's manner around you, Ruth. Shouldn't I look out for your future? His eyes tell the whole story when he sees you returning from the fields."

"He greets me in the same manner he does all his maid-servants. 'God be with you,' he says."

"Do you think a man in his fifties can court a young widow from Moab without tongues wagging? The women would think you a harlot and him an old fool. And the men . . . well, we won't talk about what they would think. Boaz won't show himself under any circumstances other than those called upon by our Law." Leaning forward, Naomi clasped Ruth's hands and smiled broadly. "But the Law is on our side."

Ruth looked confused. "I don't understand."

"Boaz is a close relative of ours, and he's been very kind by letting you gather grain with his workers. He is a compassionate man and would show mercy to anyone in need. But because he is also our close relative, he can be our family redeemer."

"Family redeemer?"

"God provided a way for widows under His Law. As our family redeemer, Boaz would take you as his wife and give you a son to carry on the name of Mahlon and inherit Elimelech's portion of the land God promised."

Ruth's face flooded with color. "After all he's done for us already, should we ask him to give me a son to carry on another man's name? What of his own inheritance?"

"Would it change anything to leave the man be? Boaz has no sons, Ruth. Nor any prospects for begetting them."

"And you think I should . . ." She stopped, stammered, blushed. "H-he's one of the elders! Surely he already knows he holds the position of our family redeemer. He hasn't offered because it isn't a responsibility he wants."

"The man is too humble to offer. What would he say to you, my dear? 'I want to offer my services . . .'? Never in a million years would he say such a thing, nor God allow it. I know Boaz better than you do. I remember him from years past, and I've listened to all that my friends have said about him in the years between. He will *never* approach you about this matter."

"Because I'm not worthy to be the wife of such a man!"

"No. Because he's more than thirty years older than you. And because, if I know him at all, he's waiting for a young man, handsome and with a charmed tongue, to offer you marriage instead." God forbid. Boaz had stood back and allowed Elimelech to claim her because she'd been swayed by physical appearance and charm. Was Boaz standing back again and waiting until the other relative realized Ruth's worth? Boaz might even make himself a matchmaker! "Boaz wouldn't put himself forward if his life depended on it." Which in Naomi's eyes it did. "The man would not risk embarrassing you with an unwanted proposition."

Ruth looked away, her brow furrowed. When she looked back at Naomi, her discomfiture was clear.

"Should I help you find a husband, Ruth? Could you be happily married to Boaz?"

Ruth considered for a long moment. "I don't know."

"Saying you don't know is better than saying a flat no," Naomi said, satisfied. "Will you trust me if I tell you that Boaz could make you happy? He would do everything in his power to make sure of it." She saw moisture build in Ruth's eyes. Before her daughter-in-law could protest, Naomi began explaining her plan. "I happen to know that tonight he will be winnowing barley at the threshing floor. Now do as I tell you—take a bath and put on perfume and dress in your nicest clothes. Then go to the threshing floor, but don't let Boaz see you until he has finished his meal. Be sure to notice where he lies down; then go and uncover his feet and lie down there. He will tell you what to do."

Ruth's face was white, her eyes wide. "Should I do such a bold thing?"

"Trust me, my daughter. Unless you make it known to the man that you want him for a husband, he'll live out his life the way he is. Should such a man go down to Sheol without sons of his own?"

"And what of you?"

"Me? What about me?"

"If Boaz does take me for his wife, what will happen to you? Should I leave you alone in this cave?"

Naomi's heart softened. Precious girl! Ruth was a jewel with many facets. Naomi was all the more determined to see her in the proper setting. "Boaz gave you a double portion the first day he met you. Do you think he would leave me out in the cold to fend for myself?" She shook her head and smiled. "If all goes as I've prayed, we will all have a future and a hope, Ruth. If the plan succeeds, it will be because God makes it so and not because an old widow has done a bit of matchmaking."

Ruth let out her breath slowly. "All right," she said slowly and inclined her head. "I will do everything you say."

Lowering her head, Naomi was silent a moment, disturbed by Ruth's solemnity. Ruth was in the springtime of her life; Boaz, autumn. Naomi could understand Ruth's hesitation, but she was certain Boaz could make her daughter-in-law happy. Still, she pondered. Would this please God, or was she making plans of her own as she had done before?

What am I to do, Lord? Many are the plans of women, but Your will prevails.

Be merciful, Jehovah-rapha. Let us all be healed of our grief and know love again. Let the homeless have a home again, a home where You are master. Boaz will teach my daughter the way of life and uphold her on her journey. I see the loneliness in the man's eyes, Jehovah-jireh. I see the love there, too. If it be Your will, soften his heart toward Ruth and her heart toward him. If they come together only out of mutual respect and duty, if it please You, Lord, let those feelings grow into love. Build a fire in each of them that will warm them for a lifetime.

+ + +

Boaz had the sheaves of barley loaded onto donkeys and carried to the high place near Bethlehem that he'd turned into a threshing floor. Shamash and the young men broke the bundles open and cast the stalks onto the hard-packed earth, where a pair of oxen were driven in a circle, dragging behind them a heavy wooden sledge. The stones fastened to the underside of the sledge crushed the stalks and loosened the grain. Girding his loins, Boaz joined his servants in the work. The air filled with the scents of crushed stalks, oxen, and the hot sun and earth. When the floor was heavy with broken stalks of barley, the oxen were led away and the men took up their winnowing forks.

Boaz pitched grain into the air. The afternoon breeze caught the straw and chaff and whiffed it away while the heavier kernels of barley dropped back to the threshing floor. It was hot, hard work. Over and over, he dug his fork into the piles of threshed grain. Sweat soaked through his tunic and beaded on his forehead. He paused and tied a cloth around his head to keep the perspiration from dripping into his eyes. Bending to his labor, he raised a song of celebration and his servants joined in.

As the threshing progressed, he set workers to gather the straw into piles to be stored and used through the year to fire stoves and feed his animals. When the bits of straw and chaff were too small to be pitched by fork, the men set aside their winnowing forks and used shovels instead. They paused to eat and drink and then returned to work. When the breeze died down, some of the servants waved woven mats to blow the chaff from the barley. Other workers began to purify the grain by sifting. As the grain passed through, bits of rubbish were caught in the sieves and thrown away. The darnel grains were removed, for if these weed and tare seeds were left, they would be eaten and cause dizziness and sickness.

The harvest was so plentiful, the work would last for several days. "Enough for today, men!" Boaz called out. His cooks were ready with savory dishes of bean-and-lentil stew. Trays of fruit were set out, along with plenty of bread and wine. The men relaxed, talked, sang, and laughed as the stars came out.

No lanterns were lit, for the risk of fire was too great.

✦   ✦   ✦

Ruth sat some distance from the threshing floor and watched Boaz sing, laugh, and drink with his servants. When the stars came out, she moved closer as the celebrating slowed. When Boaz rose, the gathering broke up. His servants spread out and found places to cover themselves with their mantles for sleep. Work would begin again early in the morning. Ruth watched Boaz lie down beside the pile of grain.

She remained concealed in an outcropping of rocks for another hour. She wanted to be certain all of Boaz's servants had settled down for the night and were asleep before she came out of her hiding place. She couldn't risk being seen here. Gossip would spread through Bethlehem like a fire, burning up her reputation. That thought tortured her as she moved slowly, cautiously, toward the place where Boaz slept. Her heart thumped until she felt sick with tension.

When she finally reached him, she hesitated, studying the man in the half-moon light next to the mound of grain. He looked younger, his many responsibilities forgotten in sleep. He lay with one arm flung over his head. Trembling, Ruth knelt at his feet and drew his mantle back carefully so she wouldn't disturb him. He moved restlessly. Her pulse jumped. She curled up quickly at his feet without making a sound and drew his mantle over her so that the cool night air would not awaken him. Then she released her breath slowly, wishing her heart would slow its wild, erratic pace.

She tried to make herself relax, but how could she with this man so close she could hear his breathing and feel his warmth? She could smell the sweat of his body mingled with the scents of earth, straw, and barley. She remembered how the odor of sickness and fear had clung to Mahlon during the last months of his life. The scent of Boaz's body was that of life—hard work, the fruit of his labor, the land God had given him. His essence was at once provocative and soothing.

She swallowed and closed her eyes, disturbed by the emotions this great man stirred within her. Putting her hand beneath her cheek, she listened to the sound of her own heart racing in her ears and the slow, even breathing of the man so close his feet were against her back.

+ + +

Boaz awakened in the middle of the night and lay still, wondering what had startled him. A dream? He couldn't remember it. He listened for a long moment, but nothing moved. In fact, there was an uncanny stillness around him. He heard one of the men snoring loudly from the other side of the mound of grain and relaxed. Inhaling deeply, he closed his eyes, intending to go to sleep again, but instead he came more fully awake as he smelled a sweetness in the air he breathed. He frowned slightly, attentive to it. He breathed in again and thought he had never smelled anything so luscious. Where did it come from? Was an evening breeze bringing the scent of flowers? No, it was too rich and evocative. Like perfume.

When he stretched out his leg, he brushed against someone. The interloper was small and curved. He drew in his breath sharply. Pulling his foot back abruptly, he sat up and threw off his mantle. Who but a harlot would dare come to the threshing floor?

The woman sat up quickly and turned her head toward him. It was too dark to see her face. "Who are you?" he whispered roughly. He didn't want to awaken anyone.

"I am your servant Ruth."

His heart began to hammer. *"Ruth?"* His voice came out choked and confused.

Her voice shook. "Spread the corner of your covering over me, for you are my family redeemer."

A flood of heat swept through his entire body beginning with the foot that had brushed against her body. He could hardly breathe for the nearness of her and the request she made. Never in the solitude of his wishful thinking had he ever dreamed Ruth would make such a request of him. Did she know his heart had yearned for a wife to love and care for, a wife to walk with him and give him children?

Lord, Lord, how do I ever dare hope for a girl like this? There are obstacles. Is this a test? I must do what's right rather than do what I want. And You've known since the first time I heard about this girl that my heart was softened toward her. Such a woman . . . but Lord, surely Naomi is aware of the other relative. She must know it's not my right to fulfill this duty, unless . . . oh, God, give me the strength to do what I should, even if it means seeing another woman I love walk away with another man.

"The Lord bless you, my daughter!" His voice was husky with emotion. He was glad of the darkness so she wouldn't see the longing and astonishment he felt. Did she understand the kindness she was showing him by coming to him? His head swam. He'd surrendered his hope of ever having a family of his own years ago. God was God, and for whatever reason, He had chosen not to give the blessing of a wife to him. And yet, here, in the middle of the night and cloaked in darkness, a few whispered words from Ruth made Boaz's hope for a wife and children spring to life again. He forced himself to think, to consider her actions and motives. Surely she had done it for Naomi!

"You are showing more family loyalty now than ever by not running after a younger man, whether rich or poor."

"You have been kinder to me than anyone, Boaz. Will you put your mantle over me?"

He could hear the tremor in her voice and wanted to reach out to her and reassure her. It was beyond reason that she might love him, but his heart had been fixed upon her firmly from the beginning. He wanted nothing more than to take her as his wife, but was this God's will?

"Now don't worry about a thing, my daughter. I will do what is necessary, for everyone in town knows you are an honorable woman." *None more than I,* he longed to say. "But there is one problem."

"A problem?" she said softly, distress clear in her tone.

"While it is true that I am one of your family redeemers, there is another man who is more closely related to you than I am."

"Another man?"

There was no mistaking the disappointment in her tone. When she moved closer, her hand brushed his leg. She drew back quickly, but not before his body had caught fire. He wasn't such an old man after all. The power of his feelings for her shook him. He looked around, wondering if anyone had heard them speaking. What disaster would befall her if she were to be discovered here on the threshing floor! His mind raced unwillingly toward advantages to himself if that happened. The other relative would have cause to question her purity. He might then refuse to fulfill his obligations to her on the grounds of her ruined reputation. The entire city would gossip about her and speculate on what had happened between them here tonight. There would be talk for years to come. As much as Boaz wanted her, he would not dishonor her in such a way.

Could he stand before the Lord if he allowed such a thing to happen to Ruth? Could he look into her eyes if he allowed shame to be poured on her because he wasn't vigilant to do what was right? No! He must protect her reputation, even if it meant giving her up to another man. His heart sank at the thought. Gritting his teeth, he struggled with his desire to have her for himself. But how could he overlook the Law? No matter how much he wanted Ruth, he must obey the Lord.

You know I want her, don't You, Lord? Is that why You're testing me now? Oh, Jehovah-tsidkenu, give me strength not to give in to my desire to have her. Keep me to Your path, for if I step off, I am lost! Help me show Ruth the kindness she has shown me, and establish her.

"Yes," he said to her. "There is another relative who must be consulted. Stay here tonight, and in the morning I will talk to him. If he is willing to redeem you, then let him marry you. But if he is not willing, then as surely as the Lord lives, I will marry you! Now lie down here until morning. No one must know that a woman was here at the threshing floor."

Ruth lay down at his feet again. Boaz felt her presence so acutely, his stomach hurt. He wondered if she slept, for she made no sound at all. Nor did she move. He longed to touch her, to talk with her, but withheld his hand and kept his silence.

He prayed instead.

Oh, Lord, Lord . . .

He didn't even have words for the feelings stirring so strongly in him. He was shaken by her presence, shot through with hunger for her to be his wife. How many years had it been since he'd felt like this? Not since he'd thought himself in love with Naomi. *It's been more than twenty years!*

The hope of loving Ruth made him afraid for the first time in years.

+ + +

Ruth came abruptly awake when a gentle hand brushed the hair back from her forehead. *"Shhhhh."* Boaz put his finger over his lips. He was down on one knee beside her, and it was light enough to see his smile. "Everyone's still asleep," he mouthed. Dawn was coming. It was time for her to leave before any of his servants awakened and saw her there.

"Bring your cloak and spread it out," he whispered. She followed him to the pile of barley that had been purified of all the tare seeds. "I can't send you home without a present." He shoveled grain into her shawl until there was more than a bushel and a half. Then he tied it and laid it on her back. "For Naomi."

His generosity never ceased to amaze her. She could not have carried any more. "Thank you," she whispered and looked up at him. When her eyes met his, she felt the jolt of recognition and connection. He wasn't just looking at her the way a man looked at a woman he found attractive. He looked at her as though she already belonged to him. The way he studied every detail of her face made her heart quicken. She blinked, stunned by the realization that this man, so far above her station, wanted her.

When Boaz reached out, she drew in a trembling breath.

Though she stood still, waiting for his touch, he withdrew his hand. His smile became almost fatherly, his tone faintly reproving. "May it be as God wills."

+   +   +

As soon as Ruth was out of sight, Boaz awakened Shamash. "I'm going into the city. I don't know when I'll be back."

Shamash started to rise. "Is there trouble?"

Boaz put a hand on his shoulder. "No trouble, my friend. There's a matter of business I need to take care of this morning. It can't wait."

"It must be important. I've never known you to leave the threshing floor."

Boaz had no intention of explaining. He didn't want anyone speculating about Ruth's visit to the threshing floor. By the end of the day, she would have a husband. He intended to do all he could to make certain it was him. Whether he succeeded would be up to God. He squeezed Shamash's shoulder. "Pray for me, my friend. Pray what I want is what God intends."

A quick frown flickered over Shamash's face, but he responded quickly. "May the Lord give you wisdom in every circumstance."

"From your mouth to God's ears."

Boaz strode down the road toward Bethlehem, his mind racing with the plan that had been forming in his mind.

+   +   +

Ruth was home before the sun had risen and surprised to find Naomi up and watching for her. "Have you been waiting all night for me?"

"Could I sleep on such a night? Well? What happened, my daughter?"

Uttering a mirthless laugh, Ruth lowered the grain. "It's not settled yet, Mother. Boaz told me there's another relative more closely related than he is." She kept her face averted, for she didn't want Naomi to see how disturbed she'd been by that news. "But he said not to worry; he'll take care of all the details. He said if this other man won't marry me, then he will. Boaz swore by Jehovah that he would." She couldn't hide the sudden rush of tears. "What if he can't work it out and I have to marry this other man? I don't even know who he is!"

Frowning heavily, Naomi tapped her fingertips against her lips.

Wiping the tears from her cheeks, Ruth stared. "You knew, didn't you? You knew about this other man and still sent me to Boaz?"

"I want you to have the best of men."

Did Naomi know something about this other man that made him undesirable as a husband? "Who is this man?"

"He is a man like any other man, but not the man I would have for you."

"Oh, Mother. What does it matter what you and I want? It's out of our hands now." Ruth wept, the tensions of the night taking their toll on her resolve. She wished she had never agreed to go to the threshing floor. "Weren't we doing all right by ourselves? Wasn't God providing for us each day?"

Naomi embraced her. "Oh, my sweet girl, you needn't worry. Boaz wants you!"

"How can you know that?" Perhaps she had been mistaken by what she thought she saw in his eyes.

"Look at all this! Do you think the man would have sent so much grain home with you if he were indifferent to the outcome? Just be patient, my daughter, until we hear what happens. The man won't rest until he has followed through on this. He will settle it today."

✦ ✦ ✦

Boaz strode quickly through the city streets until he came to his house. Several of his servants were up and doing chores. The house was in good order; it smelled of bread baking. "Bring me water, Avizemer, and have Yishmael bring me a new tunic, mantle, and sash."

He washed carefully and donned fresh clothing. Drawing his prayer shawl over his head, he prayed again, beseeching God for wisdom and strength to do what was right. He didn't hurry in speaking with the Lord, but remained in a chamber by himself until the sun was well up and he knew he would be at peace with the outcome, whatever it was.

When he came out of his inner chamber, his servants were huddled together, whispering. They glanced up in concern. "Yishmael, I have an errand for you." Boaz smiled at the others. "Everything is fine. Go back to your work."

They did as he bid them, but he could sense their curiosity. His mouth curved in a rueful smile. It wasn't every day their master came racing into his house in the manner he had. No wonder they were concerned. They were more accustomed to seeing him come home late in the afternoon, dusty from work, ready to wash, eat, pray calmly, and go to bed. Every day had a sameness about it.

But today was different!

He gave Yishmael the names of ten of the chief men in the city, men who were good friends and honest in their dealings with everyone. "Ask them to meet me at the gate of the city." Most of the men would be easily found at the synagogue. They often met in the morning before they began their business transactions for the day. Several might already be sitting in the gate, hearing and helping to settle disputes between citizens. "As soon as you've spoken to them, go to Naomi and Ruth, the Moabitess. They live in a—"

"I know where to find them, my lord."

"Good. Bring them to the gate right away."

Boaz went down to the marketplace to find Ruth's and Naomi's relative. He knew more than he wanted to know about the man's reputation but was determined not to judge him on gossip. He intended to present Ruth's case in a way that would test the man's character. He walked among the booths until he spotted Rishon, son of Oved, brother of Elimelech, talking with several young men while his wife scooped barley from an earthen container and poured it into an old woman's woven basket. The two women argued. Scowling, Rishon turned, said something to the older woman, and gestured impatiently. The woman turned away with a defeated frown.

Stiffening, Boaz stood still for a moment, breathing in slowly and reasoning with himself. What he witnessed was not necessarily all it seemed to be. He needed to keep his mind clear for the discussion ahead. Rishon's children were in the booth with his wife. He counted three, including the baby cradled in Rishon's widowed mother's arms.

"Rishon," Boaz called, going no closer. When the younger man turned, he beckoned. "Come over here, friend. I want to talk to you." He kept his voice casual, as though what he wanted to discuss was of no great importance to him.

Rishon came readily, blushing and looking faintly guilty. "I take it you saw that woman. She's always expecting more than—"

Boaz raised his hand to stop the flow of excuses. "It's another matter I would discuss with you."

Rishon looked visibly relieved. "Another matter? What matter?"

"Come," Boaz said, holding his hand out in welcome. "Sit with me where it's cooler." He caught the glint of speculation in Rishon's eyes when he sat down in the shade of the city gate. Rishon sat down with him. Boaz called the names of the ten men who had gathered in the gate. "Will you agree to be witnesses to whatever is decided here today?"

Each agreed and took a place close by to hear out the case and act as a witness to what was decided between the two men.

Rishon looked around at them, frowning, and then faced Boaz again. "What's this all about, Boaz?"

Boaz glanced around cautiously and saw Naomi standing in the shadows. His heart thumped heavily as he saw Ruth standing behind her. When he looked at Naomi again, she raised clasped hands before her heart, smiled faintly, and nodded.

"You know Naomi," Boaz said, extending his hand toward her. Rishon glanced at her indifferently and gave a curt nod of acknowledgment before returning his full attention to Boaz. "Naomi, who came back from Moab," Boaz said.

"So I'd heard."

And yet have shown no mercy or familial consideration, Boaz thought grimly. "She is selling the land that belonged to our relative Elimelech." Rishon's eyes started to glow, for it was prime land, close to the city. "I felt that I should speak to you about it so that you can redeem it if you wish. If you want the land, then buy it here in the presence of these witnesses."

"All right," Rishon said with a full sigh of greedy anticipation. "I'll redeem it."

✦   ✦   ✦

Ruth had never seen a more handsome man than Rishon. He was much younger than Boaz, well built, ruddy, with dark curling hair and beard. He was dressed in a fine tunic and mantle and had the manner of a man eager to find any advantage. He surveyed the gathering of elders with caution, his eyes gleaming with speculation. There was a proud tilt to his head. Though he tried to take on the posture of confidence, she sensed his discomfort, as though he expected them to confront him for some error. He was wary of this meeting with Boaz and was deferential in his manner toward the older man. Ruth had the feeling Rishon's manner was not from the heart but from the head.

Nor did she like the way her relative looked at Naomi. The man barely glanced at her mother-in-law before dismissing her from his mind, as though she was of no import.

Her heart dropped when Boaz said Naomi wanted to sell her husband's land. She clutched Naomi's arm, wanting to protest for her sake, but her mother-in-law leaned close and whispered, "Boaz knows what he's doing. Trust him."

"If you want the land, then buy it here in the presence of these witnesses," Boaz was saying. "But if you don't want it, let me know right away, because I am next in line to redeem it after you."

"All right, I'll redeem it," Rishon said eagerly.

"Good," Boaz said. Ruth felt the blood drain from her face. Had she misunderstood his feelings toward her, his desire to take her for his wife? He didn't even look in her direction or seem concerned that she would become the property of Rishon.

"It's good land," Rishon said. "It's a pity it's remained fallow for so long."

"Of course, your purchase of the land from Naomi also requires that you marry Ruth, the Moabite widow. That way, she can have children who will carry on her husband's name and keep the land in the family."

Rishon's expansiveness evaporated. "The Moabitess?" He made no attempt to hide his disappointment. He looked from Boaz to the elders gathered. His mouth tightened. "So . . ." His face darkened. "Then I can't redeem it because this might endanger my own estate."

"Such is his excuse," Naomi whispered in disgust to Ruth.

Ruth wondered what bothered Rishon most. Having to do his duty to her and provide Mahlon with an heir? Or risking that any fraction of his property might go to a child she might conceive? The people who had come to watch whispered among themselves.

"His wife wouldn't like it," someone near Ruth said.

"He should do his duty by Naomi."

"He covets the land but doesn't see any point in buying it if he has to give it back as an inheritance to Elimelech's family."

Rishon glanced around at the gathering and appeared discomforted. He untied his sandal hastily and handed it to Boaz, publicly validating the transaction. "You redeem the land; I cannot do it. You buy the land." He rose quickly and pushed his way through the gawkers.

Naomi grasped Ruth's hand tightly. "He did it!" She gave a soft laugh of pleasure. "I knew he would."

Ruth caught her breath when Boaz looked at her. Though his expression was solemn and respectful, his dark eyes held a light she had never seen before. He seemed to catch himself, for he blinked and glanced away. He stood, Rishon's sandal gripped tightly in his hand. He addressed the ten elders and the crowd that had gathered to see what was going on. "You are witnesses that today I have bought from Naomi all the property of Elimelech, Kilion, and Mahlon. And with the land I have acquired Ruth, the Moabite widow of Mahlon, to be my wife. This way she can have a son to carry on the family name of her dead husband and to inherit the family property here in his hometown. You are all witnesses today."

The ten men rose with Boaz, looking majestic in their long robes and prayer shawls and phylacteries. "We are witnesses," they said.

"We are witnesses!" the crowd joined in.

Naomi pressed Ruth toward the men. "Go," she whispered, her face aglow with excitement. "Go to him, dear."

The oldest of the elders held out his hand to Ruth. The crowd parted as she walked forward and placed her hand in his. Boaz moved to stand on the other side of him. The elder smiled at Boaz and then inclined his head to Ruth. "May the Lord make the woman who is now coming into your home like Rachel and Leah, from whom all the nation of Israel descended!" He drew Ruth forward as Boaz held out his hand. When her hand was placed in his, his fingers closed warmly around hers. The elder put his hands lightly upon their clasped hands. "May you be great in Ephrathah and famous in Bethlehem. And may the Lord give you descendants by this young woman who will be like those of our ancestor Perez, the son of Tamar and Judah."

The servant who had come for her and Naomi pressed his way hastily through the throng of people and ran down the street. People were calling out blessings to Ruth and Boaz. Men and women pressed in on them in their excitement, the men slapping Boaz on the back while the women took turns embracing Ruth and offering her fervent blessings. Boaz laughed and talked to everyone. Naomi was smiling broadly, gesticulating as she talked excitedly to the friends who surrounded her. Ruth was still stunned at the outcome. Boaz kept his hand locked around hers, keeping her close by him as the people swarmed around them offering their blessings and congratulations. The crowd followed as he brought her into the city and along the street. Overwhelmed by the throng of people celebrating around them, Ruth glanced back over her shoulder, her cheeks flushed, her heart racing. Where was Naomi? Was she coming with them?

"Ruth!" Naomi called, pushing her way through the many

well-wishers, several women accompanying her. "We must prepare for the wedding," she said, embracing her and drawing her to one side as she playfully slapped Boaz's hand. "Your bride will be ready for you this evening." Ruth found herself hustled away by Naomi, her friends, and Boaz's maidservants from the fields, all of them talking at once. Ruth could scarcely catch her breath.

She was taken to the home of Abigail, a childhood friend of Naomi. Water was brought into an inner chamber where Ruth was stripped of her worn dress. She was washed thoroughly and rubbed with scented oils, her waist-length hair brushed until the thick, curling mass shone.

A young serving girl came for Naomi. "Boaz has sent gifts for Ruth to wear." They disappeared from the room, returning within moments. Naomi carried a carved box inlaid with ivory. "Look," she said as she opened it for Ruth. "Jewels! See how he prizes you." She lifted out a necklace set with red sardius, emeralds, sapphires, and diamonds. "And he's sent wedding clothes as well."

Naomi gave the box to Abigail and helped Ruth dress. "You will look like a queen." When the long white tunic was slipped over her head, Ruth sighed. She had never felt anything so soft in her life. There was an overdress as well, embroidered in vibrant colors, and a sash made from the finest gold, blue, purple, and scarlet linen thread woven into an intricate design. There were bracelets and earrings, with stones of every color of the rainbow, and a narrow crown of gold on which were loops of chains with circles of gold.

One of Abigail's handmaidens braided Ruth's hair with

the precious stones Boaz had sent. Last, a diaphanous veil edged with embroidered grapes and leaves and bundles of wheat was draped over her head. The cloud-light material hung all the way to her knees.

"The men will be coming soon," Naomi said, holding Ruth's hand and kissing it. Her eyes were shiny with tears. "I am so happy for you."

Ruth grasped Naomi's hand in both of hers. "For both of us."

Naomi caressed her cheek. "Don't be afraid of him, dear. I would not have sent you to him if I weren't convinced he could make you happy."

Quick tears filled Ruth's eyes. "But will I make him happy?"

"Oh, my sweet one. Did you not see his face when Rishon handed him the sandal? Gold and silver couldn't have pleased him more. You are his treasure, my daughter, a gift from God."

Ruth bowed her head and closed her eyes. She was shaken by Naomi's words. Could Boaz truly love her so much? Surely a man like Boaz deserved to be loved in return. But was she capable of giving him what he must long for more than anything? Would her heart soften toward him as it had toward Mahlon? Would she tremble at his touch? Would she come to yearn for the sight of him? She admired Boaz. She had the greatest respect for him. But love? Could she give her heart and her body without reservation? Would she respond to him in a way to bring him joy? Or would she always see him as a kindly father or an older brother whom she admired?

Oh, Lord God, I don't want to cause Boaz grief. Please mold me into the woman intended for this man. I have seen his wholehearted love for You. Please fill me with wholehearted love for him! Mold me into a wife who will add to his crown. I would rather die than cause this man pain!

She felt Naomi's hands upon her head, light and reassuring, and heard her pray in a soft but fervent whisper, "Oh, God of Israel, still the fears of my child. She belongs to You as I do. Please bless Ruth for her love and obedience to me. And if it be not too much to ask, give her a love for Boaz that will exceed the love she had for Mahlon . . ." her voice broke softly, "my son." She kissed Ruth on the head.

+ + +

Boaz had never been more nervous. He tried to hide it, but he noticed the smiles his servants exchanged and knew he was doing a bad job of it. He laughed in self-mockery. "I cannot even tie this sash properly!"

Shamash stepped forward. "If you will allow me, my lord?" Boaz relinquished the sash thankfully and sighed in relief when his overseer finished securing it. Another servant held a white mantle with purple, blue, and red trim. Boaz fixed the gold brooches linked by a gold chain to hold the mantle in place. Last, a gold crown studded with precious stones was placed upon his head.

His friends were gathering and filling the house. Some took delight in teasing him while others took this opportunity to praise his bride.

"It's about time you got yourself a wife, Boaz!"

"He had to trick a relative to do it!"

"Ruth is a young woman worthy of praise, my friend."

"She will fill your house with children."

"A pity such a pretty girl has to marry such an old goat!"

Boaz laughed with them, but he did not possess the confidence he displayed. How did Ruth perceive him? He wasn't young and he had never been handsome. He could think of nothing to commend himself to a young woman of virtue. Doubts assailed him from all sides, despite the joyous atmosphere surrounding him.

"Do not frown so, Boaz," Shamash said. "You'll scare the poor girl."

Boaz forced a smile. His house was overflowing with friends, including the chief men of the city. He had given orders for all the preparations, even seeing that those less fortunate had festive clothing to wear for the occasion. Everything was in readiness, except for him.

"What troubles you, Boaz?" Shamash said.

Boaz had chosen his overseer to act as his companion for the wedding ceremony. Shamash had proven himself a trusted friend over the years. Boaz drew him aside and confessed his gravest concerns. "I compelled her into this marriage. What was I thinking? I should have arranged a better match for her than—"

"A better match? There is no better match! Is it not enough that the girl respects you?"

Should he be encouraged by such words? "I want more for Ruth than that."

"Many men begin with less." Shamash smiled wryly. "Besides, it's too late to worry about all this. You *are* her husband. The covenant between you was witnessed by everyone at the gate. It's dusk and time to go and get your bride." His eyes filled with compassion. "Ruth is a young woman of wisdom, Boaz. I think you will be happily surprised at the future God has prepared for you both."

Boaz laughed nervously. "I am already happily surprised, my friend. I never thought to have a wife, let alone a wife such as Ruth."

Before leaving, Boaz made sure all the preparations for the wedding feast had been finished. The canopy was set up and decorated with flowers and boughs of greenery and lined with cushions for comfort. The house was filled with the aroma of roasting meat, fresh-baked bread, spices, and flowers. Woven mats covered the floor. Trays were already laden and ready to be presented to the guests. Boaz counted the earthen containers against the far wall. "Is there enough wine?"

"Enough, my lord," Shamash said, "and the best in all Bethlehem!"

Boaz did not ask about the bridechamber. His hand-maidens had seen to its preparation.

Shamash stepped closer. "All is in readiness, Boaz. If you delay any longer, Ruth might think you've changed your mind."

Boaz walked straight from his house, and his friends fell in beside and behind him. The procession wove through the streets of Bethlehem. His companions sang. Some played double-reed pipes, lutes, and lyres. Others danced.

When Boaz reached the house of Abigail, he didn't even have to knock before the door was opened. Naomi stood before him, her face transformed. He hadn't seen her smile since she had come home from Moab. She almost looked young again, and he was reminded of the past when he had thought to make her his wife. "I have come for my bride," he said. His heart stopped when he looked past Naomi and saw the women in festive dress bringing Ruth to him in her wedding veil. He couldn't speak another word. When he reached out to her, Ruth took his hand. He felt her fingers tremble against his as he guided her to his side. He wished he could raise the veil and see her eyes. Perhaps then, he would sense what she was feeling.

Ruth and Boaz were pressed along again as the women joined the men in the procession back through the dark streets of Bethlehem. Some of the men carried torches. The women played tambourines, beat small hand drums, clinked finger cymbals, shook tingling bells, and sang with the men. Many carried oil lamps to light the way.

When Boaz entered his house, he raised his mantle and held it over Ruth as he drew her up onto the dais beneath the canopy. He was surprised and pleased that she knew exactly what to do. He walked her in a full circle several times for all the witnesses to see that she had his covering of marriage. When he stopped, Ruth didn't hesitate. She drew off her veil and draped it over his shoulder according to custom. The people declared, "The government shall rest upon his shoulder!" Naomi was smiling proudly.

Ruth settled herself beside Boaz on a cushion beneath the canopy. "I have never seen you look more beautiful, Ruth."

She glanced up at him and he smiled. Fascinated, he watched the color mount into her cheeks. "Nor I you," she said and lowered her head again.

He gave a soft laugh. "I was sorely in need of new plumage."

She took his hand in both of hers. The warmth of her touch went up his arm and spread through his body. "May God bless you for your kindness toward me."

His throat tightened. "He already has."

+ + +

When they were escorted to the bridechamber and left alone, Boaz felt like a callow youth standing in the middle of the room. He didn't know what to say to Ruth. He wanted to put her at ease, but how could he when he'd never been more nervous in his entire life? He was ill equipped to know how to please her and wished he had talked with one of his married friends. There hadn't been time! He started to pace and stopped himself. He combed his fingers through his beard. Catching himself at this nervous activity, he put his hand at his side. Thankfully, Ruth had turned away and had not seen his fumbling ineptness.

When she drew off the embroidered overdress, he felt shock at the power of his desire. "We can wait, Ruth."

"It's expected of us."

Was it resignation or willing acceptance he heard in her voice? "We can wait," he said again.

She glanced over her shoulder. Frowning slightly, she turned fully to look at him. She said nothing for a long moment, her doe-brown eyes searching his face. He wanted to hide himself from that perusal but didn't. She blinked in surprise. She came to him then, each step across the room tightening the pain in his chest. He was more vulnerable than he had been when he had sought Naomi's hand, for he hadn't loved her as deeply as he loved this young woman.

She took his hand. He couldn't find his voice. When she kissed his palm and put it against her cheek, he couldn't move.

"It's not necessary to wait, my husband," she said softly. "I came to you without compulsion."

"Naomi sent you."

She looked up at him solemnly. She searched his eyes, her own filled with strange confusion. "I chose to obey. I hoped, but never dared believe, you would find me acceptable."

He let his breath out sharply. "I hoped," he said hoarsely, "but still don't dare believe . . ." He could not finish. This girl could destroy him with a word.

Her eyes glistened with moisture. She reached up and cupped his face. "So that you will know I belong to you, my lord." She drew his head down and kissed him.

+   +   +

And the women were saying . . .

"It's about time Boaz took a bride."

"And such a lovely girl."

"I've never seen a girl more dedicated to her mother-in-law."

"I should be so lucky!"

"Ruth is better than a son."

"Don't I know it. A son marries and forgets all about his poor old mother."

"That's some roof Ruth's put over Naomi's head."

"I should be so lucky!"

"A girl like that, I've been praying for one for my son, but he's more interested in what a girl looks like than her integrity."

"What a pity if Boaz has no real love for Ruth."

"A marriage of obligation is a cold bedfellow."

"May God give them every happiness."

The women agreed and each went her own way, returning to her own house and family.

+ + +

And the men were saying . . .

"I knew by Boaz's manner that it was something of great importance to him. He was in a great hurry to settle the matter without delay."

"Rishon didn't have a chance."

"Rishon had all the chance he deserved. He wanted the land but not the responsibility that came with it."

"Don't be so quick to cast stones. Rishon's wife has born him three daughters. Would you be so eager to give up your firstborn son for another man's inheritance? And what if his first wife bears no sons at all? What then?"

"All that aside, Rishon still neglected his duty to Naomi and Ruth."

"She is a fine girl."

"May God grant her many sons."

"Boaz has remained all these years without a wife. It will be a difficult adjustment."

"I should be so lucky!"

Some laughed.

"She is very young. I wouldn't want to see my friend's heart broken at this stage of his life."

"Your fears are without cause. Ruth is young, but her character is proven."

"I don't doubt her character. I merely pray she will love him as he most evidently loves her."

"May the Lord God of Israel warm her heart toward our friend."

RUTH gave birth nine months after the wedding festivities. Sinking back and resting against the bedding, she watched Naomi take the infant and wash him, salt him, and carefully wrap him in swaddling clothes. "He is beautiful," Naomi wept, holding him close. "So beautiful." She carried him from the room and Ruth turned her face to the wall, tears spilling silently.

Boaz came to her later. She had risen from her bed, dressed, and was sitting in the doorway to the garden, watching Naomi walk around with the baby. Boaz drew up a stool and sat beside her. "Naomi will no longer be called Mara."

Ruth looked at him. He was gazing into the garden as she had, but she couldn't read the expression on his face. "Thank you," she said softly.

He didn't look at her. "Don't thank me for doing what was right." His voice was rough with emotion.

"You have given up your firstborn son to be heir for another man's family."

"It is our way, Ruth."

"No. It wasn't Rishon's way. It is your way, Boaz. You have put others ahead of yourself."

He looked at her. "Do not praise me too highly, Ruth. I struggle between my duty and my desire." He looked away. "I am a man like any other."

She blinked back tears, wanting to cry out that he wasn't anything like others she had known. Not even Mahlon, whom she had loved so much, would have done what Boaz did.

"Do you want his name to be Mahlon?" Boaz said quietly, still watching Naomi sitting on a stone bench beneath an olive tree.

"Let his name be Obed." A servant.

"So be it. Naomi will never have to fear being alone in her old age," Boaz said.

"Nor will you."

Boaz rose. He touched her head lightly and then turned away, leaving her alone to watch Naomi with their son.

She kept the infant at night and rose every few hours to nurse him. She savored those times when the stillness surrounded her and she held her son close and felt his mouth tug at her breast. She caressed his soft cheek and let his fingers close tightly around her finger. Tears welled, but she blinked them back. When she was finished nursing him, she kept him close beside her on her bed. Each morning,

Naomi entered her chamber, leaned down to kiss Ruth, and then took Obed in her arms and tended him throughout the day, surrendering him for feedings only.

+ + +

"I shall never be called Mara again," Naomi said, laughing at the expressions crossing Obed's face. "Never again."

"He is beautiful!" the women exclaimed as they admired the baby. Every phase of Obed's growth was met with proclamations by the women of the town who often gathered at Boaz's house to watch the baby progress. "Praise the Lord who has given you a family redeemer today!"

"May he be famous in Israel."

"May this child restore your youth and care for you in your old age."

"And no doubt he will, for he is the son of your daughter-in-law who loves you so much."

"Ruth has been better to you than seven sons!"

Ah, yes, Ruth, her precious Ruth. Naomi smiled, lifting Obed to her shoulder and rubbing his back, delighting in the way the baby nuzzled against her neck and melted against her. She couldn't remember a happier time in her life than now, with this child in her arms. God had stripped her bare and now was rebuilding her house on a firm foundation. This child who had been born to replace her sons and husband would be brought up by Boaz, a man of faith, who studied the Law with diligence and passion, a man who sat in the city gate and ruled his people with wisdom and loving-kindness.

"Ah, my little one," she said, lifting Obed and kissing him beneath his chubby chin. "May you grow to be the man your father is." She delighted in her grandson's baby chuckles. As she turned, she saw Ruth watching her from the doorway, and the mother hunger was plain to see. Naomi felt a pang of conscience at the gift she had been given so willingly. Had she ever thought of the cost to Ruth? and to Boaz? Her daughter-in-law smiled and then turned away to some chore within the house. Naomi frowned slightly as she nestled Obed against her shoulder once more.

Something was missing. Naomi knew what it was, but she could do nothing about it. And so she prayed and prayed and prayed unceasingly for that which only God could give to the two who had given up so much.

✦   ✦   ✦

Ruth found it a consuming job to run Boaz's considerable household, but she was thankful for the work that occupied her time and her mind. Boaz encouraged her to make all the decisions involved in running the home, and she sought Naomi's advice frequently, gradually adapting to her new role as the wife of one of Bethlehem's leading men. She learned to delegate duties to the servants rather than try to do everything herself. She praised their work, thankful for their increasing efforts. They seemed eager to please her, and she was equally eager to see to their needs. She rose before dawn to prepare breakfast for her household and to make plans for the day's work for the servants. She watched for the best bargains in the marketplace and was generous to those in need. No one in her household went wanting. Her hand was always open, for everything Boaz touched seemed to bring forth bounty.

When Boaz had come for her at Abigail's house and taken her home with him, almost two years ago now, she'd been afraid she would disappoint him, that she would be unable to love him as he deserved to be loved. But all that had changed when he treated her with such tender respect on their wedding night. Who would not love such a man? Over the months, her feelings had blossomed and deepened even more until a miracle had happened. Having never expected to love again, she now found herself so deeply in love with Boaz that she had to remind herself he had married her only to raise up a son for her first husband.

She and Naomi spent many hours together combing flax and weaving cloth so they would have material to sew clothing for the poor, while Obed played on the floor close by. They laughed at his antics, for he was a delightful, happy baby. He kept them both occupied when he began first to crawl and then to toddle about the house, his hands ready to touch anything and everything within his reach. Sometimes Boaz would come home and watch him play, but he only held him when Naomi placed the child in his arms. It was as though Boaz waited for permission to hold his own son.

Even with all she had to do, Ruth felt a vague disquiet, an aching loneliness. She had been married to Boaz for almost two years and knew as little of his inner thoughts now as she did on the day she met him in the field of barley. He was her husband, and yet he withheld himself from her.

"I don't think he's happy," she said to Naomi one day when her mother-in-law chanced to mention how much time Boaz was spending with the other elders at the city gate.

"What gives you such a thought?"

"He rises before I do, prays alone in the garden, and leaves for the rest of the day. He spends more time with the other men than he does in his own house, Mother. Sometimes I wonder . . ."

"Wonder what?"

"If he's avoiding me."

Naomi rose and hurried over to pick up Obed before he could pull over a pile of dried flax. She laughed and scolded him, before turning back to Ruth. "Have you talked with Boaz about this?"

"How dare I speak to Boaz about anything, Mother? After all he's done for both of us, should I expect more of him?" She concentrated on her weaving, afraid to confide too much to Naomi. The last thing she wanted to do was risk hurting her mother-in-law by admitting how much she loved her husband. Would Naomi feel she was being disloyal to her dear Mahlon?

Naomi smiled slightly, balancing Obed on her hip. "Things have changed, haven't they?"

"Changed?"

"You agreed to go to Boaz so he might give you a son to claim Mahlon's inheritance. You went to Boaz so I would have a roof over my head. You went because I sent you."

"I agreed to go to him." Ruth's mouth trembled. She didn't want her mother-in-law to think she had been completely selfless in her actions. If she hadn't admired Boaz, she would not have agreed so readily to offer herself to the man. She pressed her lips together. "You know how much I loved Mahlon, Mother. You know, don't you?"

Naomi looked bemused for a moment, and then her eyes

cleared suddenly and widened. "Oh, my dear." She set Obed down. She came and sat close beside her. "You were a wonderful wife to my son. I know that better than anyone."

Ruth's hands shook as she clasped them in her lap. "I don't want to hurt you."

Naomi put her hands over Ruth's. "If you're trying to tell me you love Boaz, I can assure you I won't see it as any disloyalty to my son. In truth, I will rejoice over an answered prayer!"

"You will?" She searched Naomi's face and saw no pain at all, not even a hint of it.

Naomi cupped her cheek. "Oh, Ruth, I love you as I would a daughter of my own flesh. I want you to be happy. And Boaz is a good man, a very good man."

Ruth smiled tremulously. "A wonderful man." She felt relieved of her guilt, but it didn't change the dilemma in which she found herself. "But I think he married me for no other reason than to fulfill his duty as our relative."

"I'm sure you are mistaken. Boaz loves you. Didn't I tell you so before I sent you to him?"

"He scarcely looks at me. He hasn't touched me since . . ." She shook her head, disheartened. She swallowed hard and continued bluntly. "Boaz has succeeded in performing his duty as our relative, Mother."

"Ah," Naomi said, her eyes revealing her understanding.

Ruth glanced away. What of Boaz's inheritance? If he died without additional sons, all of his property, as well as Mahlon's, would go to Obed. A good and loving man like Boaz deserved sons to carry on his own name.

He withheld himself from her in so many ways, and she

longed to know everything about him. She wanted to share his thoughts, his pain, his struggles, his hope. But he seemed to retreat to his work, his obligations to the people of Bethlehem, his service to the Lord, anything and everything that kept him away from his own home—and his own wife. Yet how could she complain? Everyone benefited. Boaz's good deeds extended to everyone, including her and Naomi. He poured himself out for her sake and Naomi's and expected nothing for himself. He didn't seem to expect—or even want—her love.

Ruth felt confined, trapped in silence. She was so confused, her emotions in such turmoil. She hadn't felt this uncertainty when she left Moab. She had come to Bethlehem, content to spend the rest of her life taking care of her beloved mother-in-law. Instead, God had taken her beneath His mighty wing and provided for her through the kindness of Boaz. Why should she, the lowest of the low in Bethlehem, a foreigner, be elevated before all eyes and made the wife of the kindest, most generous, most righteous man in all the city? She rejoiced daily over the blessings God had poured upon her, even while feeling increasingly unworthy of them.

So why this unending sorrow? How dare she ask for more? And yet . . . how she longed to make her husband happy!

Oh, Boaz, my Boaz!

She spent her days waiting for him to return home. She melted when he smiled at her, even if it was a fatherly smile. Just the sound of his voice made her heart sing. When he touched her, she trembled.

But Boaz was at home less and less. And she could think of only one reason why he would absent himself so much of the time. He could not return her feelings and felt uncomfortable in her company. For surely he had sensed how deeply she loved him.

She had prayed that God would make her content to spend the rest of her life on the periphery of her husband's life, content in his contentment. She wanted to be a part of Boaz's life, wanted him to trust her enough to share his struggles and triumphs, wanted to be part of *him*. But it seemed that Boaz didn't share her desire.

"What is it, my daughter?" Naomi said, holding Ruth's hand between her own. "What is causing you such grief?"

"I love him. I love him so much it hurts." She loved him more than she had ever loved anyone, even Mahlon.

"And you haven't told him."

"I don't want to embarrass him."

"Embarrass him? Is it better if he thinks he's failed as a husband?"

Ruth drew back. "He hasn't failed!"

"Anyone can see you're unhappy."

"Because he stays away, Mother." She rose from her loom and moved away, restless. "Because he's never home."

"My dearest Ruth, a man who marries late in life has little knowledge of how a woman thinks, let alone a young woman in love. He probably stays away because he believes it will make you happy."

Ruth blinked and looked back at Naomi. She'd never considered that.

"Boaz is only a man, my dear, and men are not always as

strong as they portray themselves. I imagine Boaz thinks of himself as a much older man than his lovely young wife, too old for her to love. You could crush his heart with a word."

"I want to make him happy."

Naomi smiled. "Then accept this old woman's blessing, and *do so*."

+   +   +

Naomi was not content to leave things as they were. Her daughter-in-law had been bold once for her sake, but Naomi doubted she would have the confidence to reach out and grab hold of anything for herself. Naomi left the house soon after speaking with Ruth. She said she was going to visit a sick friend. She made her way straight to the city gate, where she knew she would find Boaz. He was there, as usual, and in his usual place. He saw her coming and looked troubled, even more so when she beckoned him. With a word to the other chief men, he rose and came to her. "Is something wrong?"

"All is well," she said.

"Then why do you look the way you do?"

"What way do I look?"

"Like a woman ready to do battle."

He was blind only when it came to his young wife. "Can we walk together and talk somewhere that people won't be listening to our every word and watching our every move?"

Frowning, Boaz fell into step beside her, matching his pace to hers as she walked out of Bethlehem. She said nothing for a long time. Let him stew and wonder. Let him *ask*.

"Did Ruth send you?"

"No, she didn't send me. I came of my own accord. Some-one has to light a fire under you."

"A fire?"

She stopped and looked up at him. "There are times when a man can safely put his heart above his head, Boaz."

He stepped away uneasily. "What are you talking about, Naomi?"

"What do you think I'm talking about? You love her, don't you?" The color that poured into his face was all the answer she needed. She crossed her arms over her chest and glared at him. "When do you intend to tell her you married her for reasons other than honor and legal obligations?"

"She knows," he said dully.

Naomi threw her arms in the air. "And how would the girl know?" She paced back and forth in front of him. "You managed to stay home with her for the seven days of the wedding celebration, but then you dove back into your life as usual. You spend every waking hour overseeing things your overseer gets paid to oversee. And if you're not about your own business, you're tending everyone else's business at the gate. You treat Ruth like a guest in your house! She is *your wife!*"

She stopped reproaching him, satisfied with his stunned look. She pulled her shawl tightly around her and glared up at him. "I knew about Rishon, Boaz. Did you think I could spend a whole month in Bethlehem and not know about every living relative and friend I'd left behind? I didn't want Rishon to have Ruth! Would he hold her in the esteem you do? Would he love her? I watched you sitting at the city gate, and I saw the way you looked at my daughter-in-law when she was coming in from your fields. And I praised God for you and the feelings you had for her! That's why I sent Ruth to you. I sent her to you because *you loved her*."

"Yes, I love her," he said roughly. "And now you have a son to carry on Elimelech's name. What more do you want from me, Naomi?" He turned away and raked a hand back through his hair.

She let out her breath. Compassion filled her, along with an aching regret. "I want you to be happy, Boaz. I want you to accept the gift I gave you."

"I have accepted Ruth."

"No, you haven't."

He turned and looked at her, his eyes dark with pain. "Her son will have everything I own. Is that not acceptance? Does that not show how highly I esteem her—and you?"

"Ruth is in love with you, Boaz."

He stared at her. "What?" She'd never seen a man look more astounded. "What did you say?"

"I said . . . Ruth . . . is . . . in . . . love . . . with you." She spoke slowly, as she would to a child slow to understand.

"She can't be."

"Why?" Though it would hurt, she needed to speak plainly. "Because I was blind to your beauty? And you are beautiful, Boaz, beautiful in all the ways that count, all the ways that last. Ruth sees you more clearly than I ever did, my dear, dear friend. Now, it's you who must open your eyes and see the girl you married."

"Should I believe the impossible?"

"Is anything impossible with God? I have prayed for this to happen. I know a dozen others who have prayed as well. Half of Bethlehem prays for you and Ruth! Does God not hear our prayers? Do you know how many people in Bethlehem watch and wait for the Lord to bring the greatest blessing of all upon you both? *Love.* And now He has."

"I can't believe it."

"You can say this with the same mouth that praises God who performs miracles? I know of what I speak. I left her, weeping, not long ago."

"Weeping?"

"Because you're never home where you belong."

He stood a moment, silent, and then he laughed, amazed.

It was good to hear him laugh, even better to see the light in his eyes, a light she had never seen shine so brightly.

His smile softened, his eyes searching hers. "It is strange, isn't it, Naomi? I loved you once."

"And I was a thoughtless, shallow, young girl." She came close and put her hand upon his arm. "Now I'm your mother-in-law," she said with a sly grin. She gave his arm a playful slap. "So show some respect for an old woman. Go home, *my son.* Go home to my daughter, Ruth, who loves the ground you walk on."

Boaz leaned down and kissed her cheek. "May God bless you, Naomi," he said hoarsely.

Naomi watched him stride away. She shook her head in wonder that Ruth and Boaz could have so little confidence in themselves. Ah, but they had unshaken faith in God. And that was a good thing. No, it was the best thing of all. For God would never disappoint them.

Turning her back, Naomi blinked back tears as she looked out over the harvested fields. She thought of Elimelech. She thought of Kilion and Mahlon and ached with her losses. And yet, she thanked God as well, for despite their many sins, as well as her own, their names would not die out after all.

✦   ✦   ✦

Boaz's throat was tight, his heart pounding, as he entered the house. "Ruth?"

"I'm here!" She sounded surprised. When he entered the main chamber, he saw her rise and step out from behind her loom, tense and wide-eyed. "Boaz." She blushed. "You're home early."

"Do you mind?"

"Oh, no. Of course not."

He walked toward her, searching her face. Her cheeks were deeper pink than usual. Her eyes widened even more as he came closer. She lowered her head. Was he making her uncomfortable? She reached out and fingered the cloth she was weaving, then put her hand quickly at her side. He'd never seen her more nervous. But then, she was no less nervous than he.

"Have you spoken to Naomi?" Her voice was strangely constricted.

"Yes, though I can scarcely believe what she said."

She looked up at him. "What did she say?"

He was afraid of saying too much, so he said cautiously, "She said . . . you wanted to speak with me." This time there was no doubting the color in her cheeks. "I apologize. I've embarrassed you. I think she misunderstood, or I did, or —"

140

She interrupted. "No. I hoped she would talk to you."

He stared at her. "You've only to say what you wish, Ruth. Obed can have my portion."

"You have land enough for many sons, Boaz."

His heart began to pound.

Her smile was shy after saying something so bold. But she wasn't finished. She stepped closer, looking him full in the face. "I would give you as many sons and daughters as you and God will allow."

"Oh, my love." Her eyes flickered in surprise and then filled with so much hope that he no longer doubted her feelings. He gave a soft laugh. "When I heard people talking about you, when you and Naomi first arrived, I knew you were something very special. And then when you came to my field . . . it gave me pause that a man of my age could be so stirred."

She wrapped her arms around his waist and pressed herself against him, crying. Perplexed, he held her closer. She was trembling and weeping. What had he said to bring on such grief? Breathing in the incense of her hair, he thought of the night she had come to him on the threshing floor. She had worn perfume then, but he preferred her as she was now. She smelled like springtime, and she made him feel young again. "What can I say or do to make you happy?"

"I *am* happy!"

"But you're weeping."

"Yes, I am, aren't I?" She looked up and laughed, tears streaming down her cheeks. "I've never been more happy! I want to laugh and sing and dance, all because you love me."

He laughed with her, relishing the outpouring of her feelings. "I would have spoken sooner if you had given me some small hint of your own feelings."

"How could I, when I was convinced you would be embarrassed?"

"So. Are you going to tell me now that you fell in love with me at first sight?"

"No, but I admired you from the first day when you were so kind to me."

"Like a father," he said dryly.

"Only because you persisted in calling me 'daughter.'"

He cupped her cheek tenderly. "I had to remind myself daily that I was too old for you, and that it was far from appropriate for me to feel the way I did."

"So I had to come to you and propose on the threshing floor."

"And you wouldn't have done so if Naomi hadn't pressed you into it."

"I'm glad she did. May the Lord bless her forever for it!" Ruth shook her head and let out her breath softly, her smile softening. "I never thought I could love another as I did Mahlon, and what I feel for you now is so much more. Oh, Boaz, God is merciful! He is kind and generous." Tears streamed down her cheeks as she gazed up at him with adoring eyes.

Boaz cupped her face and drank in the sight of her love. "The Lord is all that and more, my love." *Oh, Lord God, You amaze me! Never would I have dared dream of having such a treasure as this.*

Leaning down, Boaz kissed Ruth with all the love he had stored for a lifetime.

+ + +

And the women were saying . . .

"I thought she was pretty before, but even more so now. Have you ever seen a more beautiful woman than Ruth?"

"It's love that's done it."

"It's the clothes. It's got to be the clothes. Anyone can be beautiful when you're married to the richest man in town."

"If you put sackcloth on that girl, she'd still shine."

"She's a lamp on a stand."

"Have you seen the way she looks at Boaz?"

"Have you seen the way *he* looks at *her?*"

The women giggled.

"I should be so lucky."

"Naomi must be proud of her matchmaking."

"A word here, a nudge there."

"Boaz didn't need much prodding."

"Are any among us more deserving? Has anyone been more generous to the poor than Boaz?"

"Has anyone shown more devotion to her mother-in-law than Ruth?"

"Ah, but it is God who has poured His blessings upon them."

"Blessed be the name of the Lord."

+ + +

And the men were saying . . .

"I rejoice at our brother's happiness!"

"As do we all, brother!"

"Boaz waited a long time for the Lord to answer his prayer."

"A good wife is more precious than rubies."

"Beauty doesn't last."

"True, but Ruth is a young woman who fears God and respects her husband."

"And loves him. Anyone with eyes can see."

"She is to be highly praised."

"May our brother's household increase."

"May their sons be like Boaz, and their daughters like Ruth!"

"From your mouth to God's ears."

And the assembly at the gate all said, *"Amen!"*

THIS is the family tree of Boaz, beginning with his ancestor Perez: Perez (whose mother was Tamar), Hezron, Ram, Amminadab, Nahshon, Salmon, Boaz, Obed, Jesse, and David, who became king of Israel. And from the line of King David came the Christ, the anointed One of God, Jesus, our Savior and Lord.

DEAR READER,

You have just read the story of Ruth as perceived by one author. Is this the whole truth about the story of Ruth, Naomi, and Boaz? Jesus said to seek and you will find the answers you need for life. The best way to find the truth is to look for yourself!

This "Seek and Find" section is designed to help you discover the story of Ruth as recorded in the Bible. It consists of six short studies that you can do on your own or with a small discussion group.

You may be surprised to learn that this ancient story will have applications for your life today. No matter where we live or in what century, God's Word is truth. It is as relevant today as it was yesterday. In it we find a future and a hope.

Peggy Lynch

SEEK GOD'S WORD FOR TRUTH
Read the following passage:

In the days when the judges ruled in Israel, a man from Bethlehem in Judah left the country because of a severe famine. He took his wife and two sons and went to live in the country of Moab. The man's name was Elimelech, and his wife was Naomi. Their two sons were Mahlon and Kilion. They were Ephrathites from Bethlehem in the land of Judah. During their stay in Moab, Elimelech died and Naomi was left with her two sons. The two sons married Moabite women. One married a woman named Orpah, and the other a woman named Ruth. But about ten years later, both Mahlon and Kilion died. This left Naomi alone, without her husband or sons.

Then Naomi heard in Moab that the Lord had blessed his people in Judah by giving them good crops again. So Naomi and her daughters-in-law got ready to leave Moab to return to her homeland. With her two daughters-in-law she set out from the place where she had been living, and they took the road that would lead them back to Judah.

But on the way, Naomi said to her two daughters-in-law, "Go back to your mothers' homes instead of coming with me. And may the Lord reward you for your kindness to your husbands and to me. May the Lord bless you with the security of another marriage." Then she kissed them good-bye, and they all broke down and wept.

"No," they said. "We want to go with you to your people."

But Naomi replied, "Why should you go on with me? Can I still give birth to other sons who could grow up to be your husbands? No, my daughters, return to your parents' homes, for I am too old to marry again. And even if it were possible, and I were to get married tonight and bear sons, then what? Would you wait for them to grow up and refuse to marry someone else? No, of course not, my daughters! Things are far more bitter for me than for you, because the Lord himself has caused me to suffer."

And again they wept together, and Orpah kissed her mother-in-law good-bye. But Ruth insisted on staying with Naomi. "See," Naomi said to her, "your sister-in-law has gone back to her people and to her gods. You should do the same."

But Ruth replied, "Don't ask me to leave you and turn back. I will go wherever you go and live wherever you live. Your people will be my people, and your God will be my God. I will die where you die and will be buried there. May the Lord punish me severely if I allow anything but death to separate us!" So when Naomi saw that Ruth had made up her mind to go with her, she stopped urging her.

RUTH 1:1-18

There are many life-changing events that come into our lives. List all the life-changing events you find in the above passage.

How many of these events were the result of Naomi's choices?

What is her response to these events?

What do you learn about Naomi's daughters-in-law?

What choices did they make?

With whom do you identify?

FIND GOD'S WAYS FOR YOU
What life-changing events have you experienced?

Who helped you through these events?

What kind of counsel did you receive?

Naomi and Ruth needed wisdom to make their decisions. Contrast worldly wisdom and godly wisdom from the following passage:

> If you are wise and understand God's ways, live a life of steady goodness so that only good deeds will pour forth. And if you don't brag about the good you do, then you will be truly wise! But if you are bitterly jealous and there

is selfish ambition in your hearts, don't brag about being wise. That is the worst kind of lie. For jealousy and selfishness are not God's kind of wisdom. Such things are earthly, unspiritual, and motivated by the Devil. For wherever there is jealousy and selfish ambition, there you will find disorder and every kind of evil.

But the wisdom that comes from heaven is first of all pure. It is also peace loving, gentle at all times, and willing to yield to others. It is full of mercy and good deeds. It shows no partiality and is always sincere. And those who are peacemakers will plant seeds of peace and reap a harvest of goodness.   JAMES 3:13-18

STOP AND PONDER
Based on your contrast of wisdom from the passage you just read, which kind of wisdom do you seek? Which kind of wisdom do you impart to others?

provisions

SEEK GOD'S WORD FOR TRUTH
Read the following passage:

> So the two of them continued on their journey. When they came to Bethlehem, the entire town was stirred by their arrival. "Is it really Naomi?" the women asked.
>
> "Don't call me Naomi," she told them. "Instead, call me Mara, for the Almighty has made life very bitter for me. I went away full, but the Lord has brought me home empty. Why should you call me Naomi when the Lord has caused me to suffer and the Almighty has sent such tragedy?"
>
> So Naomi returned from Moab, accompanied by her daughter-in-law Ruth, the young Moabite woman. They arrived in Bethlehem at the beginning of the barley harvest.
>
> RUTH 1:19-22

When Ruth and Naomi arrive in Bethlehem, how are they received?

What is Naomi's attitude? Whom does she blame for her misfortunes?

Read the following passage:

> Now there was a wealthy and influential man in Bethlehem named Boaz, who was a relative of Naomi's husband, Elimelech.
>
> One day Ruth said to Naomi, "Let me go out into the fields to gather leftover grain behind anyone who will let me do it."
>
> And Naomi said, "All right, my daughter, go ahead." So Ruth went out to gather grain behind the harvesters. And as it happened, she found herself working in a field that belonged to Boaz, the relative of her father-in-law, Elimelech.
>
> RUTH 2:1-3

Describe Ruth's plan to take care of her mother-in-law.

Who owned the field where she worked? Who was he?

Read the following passage:

> Boaz went over and said to Ruth, "Listen, my daughter.
> Stay right here with us when you gather grain; don't go to
> any other fields. Stay right behind the women working in
> my field. See which part of the field they are harvesting,
> and then follow them. I have warned the young men not
> to bother you. And when you are thirsty, help yourself to
> the water they have drawn from the well."
>
> Ruth fell at his feet and thanked him warmly. "Why
> are you being so kind to me?" she asked. "I am only a
> foreigner."
>
> "Yes, I know," Boaz replied. "But I also know about the
> love and kindness you have shown your mother-in-law
> since the death of your husband. I have heard how you left
> your father and mother and your own land to live here
> among complete strangers. May the Lord, the God of
> Israel, under whose wings you have come to take refuge,
> reward you fully."
>
> "I hope I continue to please you, sir," she replied. "You
> have comforted me by speaking so kindly to me, even
> though I am not as worthy as your workers."   RUTH 2:8-13

What did the landowner offer her and why?

What is Ruth's response?

FIND GOD'S WAYS FOR YOU

When you are faced with life's misfortunes or even the everyday "calamities," how do you respond?

Whom do you blame? Why?

Do you identify with either Ruth or Naomi? Why?

Read the following verse:

> Work with enthusiasm, as though you were working for the Lord rather than for people.   EPHESIANS 6:7

Ruth accepted the circumstances that had placed her in a humbling, subservient position. What does Ephesians 6:7 say about serving?

STOP AND PONDER
Read Ephesians 6:7 again. What kind of servant are you?

SEEK GOD'S WORD FOR TRUTH
Read the following passage:

> Boaz arrived from Bethlehem and greeted the harvesters.
> "The Lord be with you!" he said.
>
> "The Lord bless you!" the harvesters replied.
>
> Then Boaz asked his foreman, "Who is that girl over
> there?"
>
> And the foreman replied, "She is the young woman from
> Moab who came back with Naomi. She asked me this
> morning if she could gather grain behind the harvesters.
> She has been hard at work ever since, except for a few
> minutes' rest over there in the shelter.". . .
>
> At lunchtime Boaz called to her, "Come over here and
> help yourself to some of our food. You can dip your bread
> in the wine if you like." So she sat with his harvesters, and
> Boaz gave her food—more than she could eat.
>
> When Ruth went back to work again, Boaz ordered his

young men, "Let her gather grain right among the sheaves without stopping her. And pull out some heads of barley from the bundles and drop them on purpose for her. Let her pick them up, and don't give her a hard time!"

So Ruth gathered barley there all day, and when she beat out the grain that evening, it came to about half a bushel. She carried it back into town and showed it to her mother-in-law. Ruth also gave her the food that was left over from her lunch.

"So much!" Naomi exclaimed. "Where did you gather all this grain today? Where did you work? May the Lord bless the one who helped you!"

So Ruth told her mother-in-law about the man in whose field she had worked. And she said, "The man I worked with today is named Boaz."

"May the Lord bless him!" Naomi told her daughter-in-law. "He is showing his kindness to us as well as to your dead husband. That man is one of our closest relatives, one of our family redeemers."

Then Ruth said, "What's more, Boaz even told me to come back and stay with his harvesters until the entire harvest is completed."   RUTH 2:4-7, 14-21

In the previous lesson, we read that Boaz was "a wealthy and influential man." What evidence do you find in this passage to support that statement?

What report did Boaz receive from his foreman regarding Ruth?

What did Boaz offer Ruth and why?

Why do you think Boaz gave special orders to his young men regarding Ruth?

How did Naomi respond to Boaz's provision?

FIND GOD'S WAYS FOR YOU
What does it mean to you to have character?

Difficult situations in life reveal our real character. What kind of report could be given about you?

What opportunities have you had to encourage people less fortunate than yourself? How have you treated them?

Read the following passage:

> Dear brothers and sisters, what's the use of saying you have faith if you don't prove it by your actions? That kind of faith can't save anyone. Suppose you see a brother or sister who needs food or clothing, and you say, "Well, good-bye and God bless you; stay warm and eat well"— but then you don't give that person any food or clothing. What good does that do?
>
> So you see, it isn't enough just to have faith. Faith that doesn't show itself by good deeds is no faith at all—it is dead and useless.
>
> Now someone may argue, "Some people have faith; others have good deeds." I say, "I can't see your faith if you don't have good deeds, but I will show you my faith through my good deeds." JAMES 2:14-18

According to this passage, how important are your actions toward others in need?

STOP AND PONDER

> "For I was hungry, and you fed me. I was thirsty, and you gave me a drink. I was a stranger, and you invited me into your home. I was naked, and you gave me clothing. I was sick, and you cared for me. I was in prison, and you visited me. And the King will tell them, 'I assure you, when you did it to one of the least of these my brothers and sisters, you were doing it to me!'"
>
> MATTHEW 25:35-36, 40

What would the King have to say about you?

SEEK GOD'S WORD FOR TRUTH
Read the following passage:

> One day Naomi said to Ruth, "My daughter, it's time that
> I found a permanent home for you, so that you will be
> provided for. Boaz is a close relative of ours, and he's been
> very kind by letting you gather grain with his workers.
> Tonight he will be winnowing barley at the threshing
> floor. Now do as I tell you—take a bath and put on
> perfume and dress in your nicest clothes. Then go to the
> threshing floor, but don't let Boaz see you until he has
> finished his meal. Be sure to notice where he lies down;
> then go and uncover his feet and lie down there. He will
> tell you what to do."
>
> "I will do everything you say," Ruth replied. So she
> went down to the threshing floor that night and followed
> the instructions of her mother-in-law.
>
> After Boaz had finished his meal and was in good spirits,

he lay down beside the heap of grain and went to sleep. Then Ruth came quietly, uncovered his feet, and lay down. Around midnight, Boaz suddenly woke up and turned over. He was surprised to find a woman lying at his feet! "Who are you?" he demanded.

"I am your servant Ruth," she replied. "Spread the corner of your covering over me, for you are my family redeemer."

"The Lord bless you, my daughter!" Boaz exclaimed. "You are showing more family loyalty now than ever by not running after a younger man, whether rich or poor. Now don't worry about a thing, my daughter. I will do what is necessary, for everyone in town knows you are an honorable woman. But there is one problem. While it is true that I am one of your family redeemers, there is another man who is more closely related to you than I am. Stay here tonight, and in the morning I will talk to him. If he is willing to redeem you, then let him marry you. But if he is not willing, then as surely as the Lord lives, I will marry you! Now lie down here until morning."

So Ruth lay at Boaz's feet until the morning, but she got up before it was light enough for people to recognize each other. For Boaz said, "No one must know that a woman was here at the threshing floor." Boaz also said to her, "Bring your cloak and spread it out." He measured out six scoops of barley into the cloak and helped her put it on her back. Then Boaz returned to the town.

When Ruth went back to her mother-in-law, Naomi asked, "What happened, my daughter?"

Ruth told Naomi everything Boaz had done for her, and she added, "He gave me these six scoops of barley and said, 'Don't go back to your mother-in-law empty-handed.'"

Then Naomi said to her, "Just be patient, my daughter, until we hear what happens. The man won't rest until he has followed through on this. He will settle it today."

RUTH 3:1-18

According to this passage, what is Naomi's concern for Ruth?

Describe Naomi's plan.

What evidence do you find that Ruth trusted the advice of her mother-in-law?

What did Ruth ask of Boaz when he discovered her at the foot of his bed?

What was Boaz's response, and what does he reaffirm about Ruth?

What surprising information did Boaz tell Ruth, and what did he plan to do about it?

FIND GOD'S WAYS FOR YOU
What concerns do you have for your loved ones?

What plans have you tried to make for them? How did they turn out?

How have you handled awkward situations with loved ones? What was their response?

Share how you have carried out special promises.

STOP AND PONDER

> Trust in the Lord with all your heart; do not depend on your own understanding. Seek his will in all you do, and he will direct your paths.   PROVERBS 3:5-6

Who directs you?

obligations

SEEK GOD'S WORD FOR TRUTH
Read the following passage:

> So Boaz went to the town gate and took a seat there. When
> the family redeemer he had mentioned came by, Boaz
> called out to him, "Come over here, friend. I want to talk
> to you." So they sat down together. Then Boaz called ten
> leaders from the town and asked them to sit as witnesses.
> And Boaz said to the family redeemer, "You know Naomi,
> who came back from Moab. She is selling the land that
> belonged to our relative Elimelech. I felt that I should
> speak to you about it so that you can redeem it if you
> wish. If you want the land, then buy it here in the pres-
> ence of these witnesses. But if you don't want it, let me
> know right away, because I am next in line to redeem it
> after you."
>
> The man replied, "All right, I'll redeem it."
>
> Then Boaz told him, "Of course, your purchase of the

land from Naomi also requires that you marry Ruth, the Moabite widow. That way, she can have children who will carry on her husband's name and keep the land in the family."

"Then I can't redeem it," the family redeemer replied, "because this might endanger my own estate. You redeem the land; I cannot do it."

In those days it was the custom in Israel for anyone transferring a right of purchase to remove his sandal and hand it to the other party. This publicly validated the transaction. So the other family redeemer drew off his sandal as he said to Boaz, "You buy the land."   RUTH 4:1-8

According to this passage, where does Boaz go and what does he do?

Initially, what does Boaz tell the next of kin? What is the relative's response?

What information does Boaz withhold at first?

What excuse does the relative offer for his change of mind?

What does the relative finally tell Boaz?

How was a transaction of this kind legalized?

FIND GOD'S WAYS FOR YOU
How do you go about making major decisions?

From whom do you draw support and wise counsel?

What excuses do you offer people when you don't want to do something?

How would you speak the truth in love? Give an example.

STOP AND PONDER

> Don't copy the behavior and customs of this world, but let God transform you into a new person by changing the way you think. Then you will know what God wants you to do, and you will know how good and pleasing and perfect his will really is.   ROMANS 12:2

Have you let God transform you?

SEEK GOD'S WORD FOR TRUTH
Read the following passage:

> Then Boaz said to the leaders and to the crowd standing around, "You are witnesses that today I have bought from Naomi all the property of Elimelech, Kilion, and Mahlon. And with the land I have acquired Ruth, the Moabite widow of Mahlon, to be my wife. This way she can have a son to carry on the family name of her dead husband and to inherit the family property here in his hometown. You are all witnesses today."
>
> Then the leaders and all the people standing there replied, "We are witnesses! May the Lord make the woman who is now coming into your home like Rachel and Leah, from whom all the nation of Israel descended! May you be great in Ephrathah and famous in Bethlehem. And may the Lord give you descendants by this young woman who will be like those of our ancestor Perez, the son of Tamar and Judah."

So Boaz married Ruth and took her home to live with him. When he slept with her, the Lord enabled her to become pregnant, and she gave birth to a son. And the women of the town said to Naomi, "Praise the Lord who has given you a family redeemer today! May he be famous in Israel. May this child restore your youth and care for you in your old age. For he is the son of your daughter-in-law who loves you so much and who has been better to you than seven sons!"

Naomi took care of the baby and cared for him as if he were her own. The neighbor women said, "Now at last Naomi has a son again!" And they named him Obed. He became the father of Jesse and the grandfather of David.

This is their family line beginning with their ancestor Perez:

Perez was the father of Hezron.
Hezron was the father of Ram.
Ram was the father of Amminadab.
Amminadab was the father of Nahshon.
Nahshon was the father of Salmon.
Salmon was the father of Boaz.
Boaz was the father of Obed.
Obed was the father of Jesse.
Jesse was the father of David.   RUTH 4:9-22

Boaz is sitting with the elders, and the relative has declined any right to Naomi's property. What does Boaz announce to this assembly of elders?

What further claim does he extend regarding Ruth?

The elders respond by saying, "We are witnesses!" What is their blessing for Boaz?

Finally, Ruth and Boaz marry. When they have a baby son, how do the townswomen react? How do they bless Naomi?

Who would this new baby's grandson be?

FIND GOD'S WAYS FOR YOU
Read the following passage:

> Then Jesus said, "Come to me, all of you who are weary and carry heavy burdens, and I will give you rest. Take my yoke upon you. Let me teach you, because I am humble and gentle, and you will find rest for your souls. For my yoke fits perfectly, and the burden I give you is light."
>
> MATTHEW 11:28-30

Who has offered to give us rest from the burdens that weary us?

A yoke is used to help oxen share a burden. What kind of yoke does Jesus offer?

What is the weight of the burden Jesus will give us?

What is the nature of Jesus' character?

STOP AND PONDER

> Jesus told him, "I am the way, the truth, and the life. No one can come to the Father except through me."   JOHN 14:6

Are you yoked to Jesus? If not, what hinders you?

THIS is a record of the ancestors of Jesus the Messiah, a descendant of King David and of Abraham:

Abraham was the father of Isaac.
Isaac was the father of Jacob.
Jacob was the father of Judah and his brothers.
Judah was the father of Perez and Zerah (their mother was **Tamar**).
Perez was the father of Hezron.
Hezron was the father of Ram.
Ram was the father of Amminadab.
Amminadab was the father of Nahshon.
Nahshon was the father of Salmon.
Salmon was the father of Boaz (his mother was **Rahab**).
Boaz was the father of Obed (his mother was **Ruth**).
Obed was the father of Jesse.
Jesse was the father of King David.
David was the father of Solomon (his mother was **Bathsheba, the widow of Uriah**).

Solomon was the father of Rehoboam.
Rehoboam was the father of Abijah.
Abijah was the father of Asaph.
Asaph was the father of Jehoshaphat.
Jehoshaphat was the father of Jehoram.
Jehoram was the father of Uzziah.
Uzziah was the father of Jotham.
Jotham was the father of Ahaz.
Ahaz was the father of Hezekiah.
Hezekiah was the father of Manasseh.
Manasseh was the father of Amos.
Amos was the father of Josiah.
Josiah was the father of Jehoiachin and his brothers (born at the time of the exile to Babylon).
After the Babylonian exile:
Jehoiachin was the father of Shealtiel.
Shealtiel was the father of Zerubbabel.
Zerubbabel was the father of Abiud.
Abiud was the father of Eliakim.
Eliakim was the father of Azor.
Azor was the father of Zadok.
Zadok was the father of Akim.
Akim was the father of Eliud.
Eliud was the father of Eleazar.
Eleazar was the father of Matthan.
Matthan was the father of Jacob.
Jacob was the father of Joseph, the husband of Mary.
Mary was the mother of Jesus, who is called the Messiah.

MATTHEW 1:1-16

FRANCINE RIVERS has been writing for more than twenty years. From 1976 to 1985 she had a successful writing career in the general market and won numerous awards. After becoming a born-again Christian in 1986, Francine wrote *Redeeming Love* as her statement of faith.

Since then, Francine has published numerous books in the CBA market and has continued to win both industry acclaim and reader loyalty. Her novel *The Last Sin Eater* won the ECPA Gold Medallion, and three of her books have won the prestigious Romance Writers of America Rita Award.

Francine says she uses her writing to draw closer to the Lord, that through her work she might worship and praise Jesus for all he has done and is doing in her life.

books by francine rivers

The Mark of the Lion trilogy
A Voice in the Wind
An Echo in the Darkness
As Sure As the Dawn

The Scarlet Thread
The Atonement Child
Redeeming Love

The Last Sin Eater
Leota's Garden
The Shoe Box

A Lineage of Grace series
Unveiled
Unashamed
Unshaken

Unspoken (Summer 2001)
Unafraid (Fall 2001)